I0817807

# The Fractured Life of Jenny McClain

Jennifer L. Kelly

This is a work of fiction. All of the characters, organizations, and events portrayed in this novel are either products of the author's imagination or are used fictitiously.

Copyright © 2016 Jennifer L. Kelly

BoxerBull Books

Cleveland, Ohio

All rights reserved.

ISBN: 0-9977764-0-4
ISBN-13: 978-0-9977764-0-9

# DEDICATION

*To all those who wonder....could there be more?*

*For Raz*
*March 18,1935-April 20, 2016*

# Chapter One

"Are you sure this is a good idea?" Jenny McClain bit at her lower lip nervously, causing her plum-colored lipstick to color her left front tooth.

"Of course, I'm sure it's a good idea." Hadley waved her hand in the air as if to dismiss the notion that any idea of hers could be a bad one. The Starbucks was busy. The line snaked through the door and out into the typically overcast afternoon of Cleveland. Jenny ran her finger back and forth nervously over the emerald green siren plastered across her white paper cup.

Hadley let out a long dramatic sigh, a rush of air blowing her wispy blonde bangs. "Listen, you said so yourself that you needed to get over Kevin. What better way than through hypnosis?"

"Had, this isn't just hypnosis. It's regression."

"Same difference. Seriously, Jenny, if I thought it could be dangerous I wouldn't have suggested it." Hadley leaned in across the table. "I told you Meara helped me with my anxiety. She's great. You'll love her. I promise."

It was Jenny's turn to let out a sigh. Hadley was right. What did she have to lose? She'd tried everything, but was still having difficulty figuring out exactly why she couldn't get over her break-up with Kevin. He wasn't anything special. Sure, they'd dated for three years. And soon she was about to turn thirty. Not that that mattered or anything. People turned thirty all the time. Only. Only she'd thought she'd be married by now. Only. She'd thought she'd have children and a family by now. Only. She thought instead of living in her cramped, two-bedroom apartment, she'd be living in her own house by now. Instead, she was more like single and *stuck*. And if she didn't get her act together soon, broke wouldn't be too far behind.

"You're right," Jenny found herself replying to her best friend. "Besides, what could one session hurt?" Although her words sounded more confident, her smile was tentative.

∞

Jenny checked her reflection in the mirrored doors of the lobby elevator. Meara's office was located in a general office building with twelve floors, just outside the city. She rubbed the lipstick off her front tooth and tried to tame the disobedient waves of her golden-brown hair. She knew it wasn't her looks that prevented her from finding a date. At Hadley's suggestion, she'd even tried a couple of those online dating sites, but all the guys were weird with a capital W. On one particularly bad date at the local Applebee's, the guy had even noted that his mother—HIS MOTHER—had helped him pick out his polo shirt and slacks for their date. *Next!*

The elevator reached the lobby and the doors slid open with a ding. She stepped inside and hit the button for the twelfth floor. The building was old and so was the elevator. It began its ascent with a jerk. Jenny returned to her brooding. It wasn't that she was dumb either. She graduated undergrad in the top ten percent of her class at Kent State University and had graduated in the top three percent of her class at the Cleveland Institute of Art. And she was successful, mostly. She kept a regular art blog and was known in the community for her designs and illustrations. She even had a small, permanent exhibit at one of her friend's galleries downtown.

The elevator creeped past the seventh floor. Apparently, it was the slowest elevator in Cleveland. Kevin's reasons had been vague at best. He had to focus on his career, he wasn't ready for the same level of commitment that she was...blah...blah...blah. Still, it was a bit of a jolt. One minute he was there and the next minute gone. *Poof!* Like smoke. Where had the last three years of her life gone? She began to struggle with creating new art. At first, she'd thought it would just take some time to adjust back to being single. But her heart wasn't in it. And Hadley had taken note.

Hadley was a free-loving, meditating, yogi. She owned her own studio—where she kindly displayed some of Jenny's art—and she had three other yogis who worked there. Despite her hippie ways, Hadley was a successful businesswoman. Not only did she teach yoga, but she also worked with local artisans and merchants to sell natural beauty products, healing crystals, and locally made, vegan clothing. After a year of Jenny fumbling through life blindly, and not producing any new—correction any remotely good—art, she'd called out her best friend. Hadley's solution was Meara, who she visited several years ago during a stressful bout when she first opened her yoga studio, finances were tight, customers were few, and Hadley was pretty freaked out. Despite her meditation and yoga, her anxiety about her potential failure had led her to seek assistance. That led her to Meara. Jenny wasn't sure how she'd found her—word of mouth? Google? But it didn't matter because whatever she did for Hadley had worked. Jenny just hoped it would work for her too.

The elevator finally came to a stop at the twelfth floor and the doors slid open. Jenny stepped into the hallway, her black stiletto boots sinking into the plush gray carpet that lined the hallway. The elevator doors closed behind her and began its descent back down to another floor. Across from the elevator was a fake, spiny-leafed green plant in a cream-colored ceramic pot. Above it was a sign with two names. The first name read Dr. William Martin, Psychotherapist with an arrow pointing to the left. The second name was Meara Stolarz, Regression Therapy with an arrow pointing to the right.

Jenny's heart pounded in her chest and she regretted wearing the bulky knit sweater that was now much too itchy. Why was she so nervous? Hadley had assured her that it was painless, but more importantly that it was informative. Her sessions with Meara had helped her get to the root cause of her anxiety—a feeling of lack that had been deeply ingrained in Hadley's so-called past lives. Jenny wasn't sure she believed in those sorts of things, but she was so used to Hadley and her angel books or chakra aligning workshops, that she hadn't discounted her friend's feelings or experiences. But this was different. This was *her* life. She supposed part of her fear was finding out something that she didn't want to know. Like what if she was a serial-killer in one of her past lives? She took a deep breath. She could turn left. Head to the psychotherapist's office and make an appointment, with a normal, run-of-the-mill medical professional. As if in response to the thought, something tugged gently at the corners of her mind. She couldn't place her finger on it, but she needed to know. Her art was important. Moving on was important. Feeling like herself again was important. Jenny let out the breath she had been holding.

She turned right.

## Chapter Two

Jenny looked around as she shut the door behind her. The reception area had a small, wicker table with a tray on top. The tray held an electric teapot, a canister of various teabags, and a stack of mismatched mugs. There were several potted plants in various stages of bloom and two ragged-looking leather chairs off to the side. A torchiere lamp with a crooked lampshade stood sentry in the corner.

The only thing the reception area was missing was an actual receptionist. Could anyone just waltz in here at any time? With the way things were nowadays—what with shootings in schools, movie theaters, even churches—the lack of security seemed unnerving. She had to remind herself of Hadley's reassurance that the experience would be a positive one.

"Hello?" A deep, female-voice called from the other side of a closed door on the wall opposite the display of tea. The door knob turned and the door pushed open. A woman in her late fifties wearing black dress slacks, patent pumps, and a loose, airy terracotta tunic opened the door. Her glasses were on a chain resting at her chest. She had auburn hair cut to her chin in a sharp, angled bob, and her brown eyes were discerning as she peered at Jenny. A look of recognition passed over her soft features. "Ah, you must be Hadley's friend, Jenny. I'm Meara."

Jenny tried to swallow her nerves and give a friendly smile. "Yeah, that's me. Hadley's friend. Jenny McClain."

"Hadley's told me a lot about you." Jenny raised an inquiring eyebrow.

"Oversouls." Meara let the door softly close behind her as she made her way to the tea table. She selected a chipped, cerulean blue mug and filled it with hot water before carefully choosing a tea bag.

"Oversouls?" Jenny asked.

Meara turned toward Jenny, her hands wrapped around the mug, and smiled. "We'll get to that in a bit. But first, I figured we should get to know one another." Her nails were painted a chocolate brown. Jenny had always thought Hadley was a bit of a hippy, dippy, *woo-woo* type. But she loved her for it, with her yoga and chakras. Hadley had been like that since they met in college at Kent. Meara was different though. She wasn't what Jenny had expected. Jenny had expected someone similar to Hadley, but older. Instead, Meara was sophisticatedly dressed, almost fashionable, yet she moved with a sort of earthy sensuality, from the way she walked to her selection of which mug to use for her tea.

"Is it really safe to not have an intercom or to leave the door unlocked like that?" She didn't want to be a worrywart, but she couldn't seem to help it.

Meara took a sip of tea and then shook her head. She made her way to one of the soft, leathered chairs and motioned for Jenny to sit in the other one. "That door used to have seven deadbolts on it. But recently, I've come to terms with my own fear-based issues and realized that when I barricaded myself in like that I was trying to be in control."

Jenny ignored the tea and sank down into the chair opposite Meara, letting her purse slide to the floor beside her. She glanced at the door and noticed the scratches and indentations from where the deadbolts used to be.

"And who's in control now?"

Meara smiled again. "Surely, not me." The peacefulness with which she said it unnerved Jenny. "Now, enough about me. Let's talk about you. Why have you come to visit me?"

When Jenny had made the appointment all that she gave Meara was her full name and phone number, as well as Hadley's recommendation, nothing else. She shifted uneasily in her seat. Why had she come? For answers. For help in letting go and moving on. For peace of mind.

She surprised herself when she replied: "Fear."

Now it was Meara's turn to raise an eyebrow. "Fear?"

The words spilled out before Jenny could seem to stop them. "Fear that I am not loveable. It's preventing me from moving on since…since my last relationship."

"And how long ago was that?"

The answer embarrassed Jenny. "Over a year ago."

"You've dated since then?" Jenny nodded. "And besides resolving this fear…is there anything else that you hope to gain from this experience?" The question wasn't meant to be prodding, but again Jenny could feel something faraway tugging at the edges of her mind. She couldn't quite put her finger on it, so she just shook her head. "Don't worry, your subconscious knows the answers to the questions you don't yet know you have." Meara stood and began walking toward the door that led out of the reception area. Jenny scrambled after her.

When they went through the door Meara paused to turn the lock. "I can't have interruptions during a client's regression. Being pulled out of a regression could have disastrous results."

Jenny felt her pulse quicken and her eyes widen. "Disastrous?"

"Only momentarily. It's quite jarring to be pulled out of one existence into another quite unwillingly." Meara led Jenny down a small hallway, past a simple bathroom on the right-hand side and toward an open door at the end of the hallway. The room was large and spacious. One entire wall was made of windows overlooking the Cleveland skyline. The wall opposite it had one of those vinyl decal sayings: *All that we see or seem, is but a dream within a dream.* She recognized the quote.

"Edgar Allen Poe? Wasn't he known as a master

of macabre?"

Meara smiled. "Actually, Poe was quite the opportunist. The images we have of him today are the result of an enemy's biographical account. In fact, he was quite the jokester, even spinning a tale about sailing in a hot air balloon in order to generate readership. If anything, I'd say he was a master of the illusion."

Jenny continued to scan the room. There was another, albeit in better condition, leather armchair and a chocolate colored chaise parallel to the window. Beneath the quote from Poe was a large, battered wooden desk with a stability ball chair. The third wall of the room was lined from ceiling to floor with overstuffed bookshelves. A candle burned on a small table near the chaise, emitting a soft, earthy scent Jenny couldn't quite place. Next to the candle was a pitcher of water and a glass.

Meara gestured at the chaise. "Please, have a seat. " She sat her mug down on the old desk, then picked up a notebook and a small, electronic device.

Jenny sat, but she didn't lie down. She wasn't quite ready yet. Meara walked over to the window and pressed a button which lowered a fabric shade partway down, so that the light of the room softened. Then she sat in the armchair next to the chaise, crossing her legs at the ankle.

"I am going to record our session today Jenny, if that's okay with you? I like my clients to be able to refer back to their sessions."

Again, Jenny nodded. Normally, she was quite chatty, but now she felt like the clichéd saying of a cat having her tongue.

"Don't worry. Soon, you'll begin to relax. It will almost be as if you're asleep, except you'll be more awake than you've ever been." Meara pushed a button on the recorder. "Okay, first, Jenny, I'll explain to you the process. Our session today will be two hours in length. First, you will lie down comfortably. Then I will walk you through a technique to convince both your mind and your body to relax. This is the hypnosis part of the regression. You will be gently guided by my voice as your mind makes its way into the Alpha brain wave state. The Alpha brain wave helps us link together states of awareness, from the subconscious to the conscious. It will feel like you are in a light sleep, almost dreaming, but believe me, you will be quite aware of what is happening. In fact, even though our session is two hours in length today, it may feel like no time has passed at all. After I am sure you are in an Alpha state of awareness, I will begin to ask you questions. All you have to do is describe to me what you see, hear, and feel."

Alpha brain waves? Subconscious and conscious awareness? This woman sounded more like a scientist than a hypnotist. "What if I don't see or hear anything?"

"Just imagine it."

"Imagine it?"

Meara nodded. "Imagination and daydreaming is the beginning awareness of the Alpha state. Pretend as if there is a door between your subconscious—I'll sometimes refer to that as your Higher Self—and your conscious. Imagination is the key that will unlock that door. Trust your initial reactions and just go with it."

Finally, Jenny voiced the fear that was nagging at her since she'd told Hadley she'd book an appointment already, if she'd just get off her case. "And what if I see something that I don't want to see?"

"The Higher Self doesn't reveal anything to us that we aren't already prepared for. This process is about trust. At any time, if you sense you are in danger, you can wake yourself up out of it. Just verbalize your desires and your conscious mind will return. It's that easy. And the session will be over."

Jenny nodded slowly as she turned her body to

the side, stretching her long legs across the chaise. Meara reached into a basket near the small table and pulled out an evergreen throw blanket which she handed to Jenny. Its softness was immediately comforting. Jenny draped it over herself before laying back and resting her head against the large microfiber pillow.

As if reading her mind, Meara added. "This session is only a little bit about trusting me, Jenny. It's about trusting yourself more than anything. Do you trust yourself?"

Jenny thought about this. She thought that she did, but maybe more importantly wasn't whether she did or didn't, but that she wanted to. "Yes."

Meara smiled. "Good. Then close your eyes."

# Chapter Three

"The sound of my voice will guide you into a deep state of relaxation. Allow your breath to become slow and even. Notice the rise and fall of your chest as you inhale the positive ions of the space around you and then exhale the negative ions out. Your breath feels cool and refreshing as you inhale. Notice as it travels through your body bringing life to each nook, cranny, and crevice. Exhale the old and tired. Inhale the new and refreshed. As your breathing slows, feel your body becoming more and more relaxed." Meara's voice was soft and smooth as she recited the words she'd committed to memory now. "As your body relaxes it grows heavy. First in your toes then moving up your calf muscles. Heavier and heavier as you sink into deeper relaxation. Next, your torso grows heavy, followed by your arms all the way from your shoulders down to your fingertips. Heavy and relaxed, your breath is slow and even. Next, relax your mind and as you do you will feel the physical sensation of heaviness."

There was a long pause. Jenny was aware of the room and she was aware of Meara's voice guiding her, but she could also feel herself growing drowsier with each of Meara's words. "Now, that you are sufficiently relaxed, we will go through the body's seven energy centers, or chakras. I want you to imagine a brilliant golden light hovering just above your head. Do you see the golden light, Jenny?"

"Yes," Jenny answered but her voice sounded far away.

"Good. Now, see that golden light entering into your crown chakra just above your head. Brilliant, warm golden light. Notice as the light travels through your skull, down your spine and into your third-eye chakra. The golden light will allow you to see what your mind does not. The golden light then travels to your throat charka. It ebbs and flows, allowing you to give voice to the unspoken. Then imagine that light reaches into your heart chakra. Beautiful, swirling yellow-gold light. As bright and warm as the sun on a clear day. It swirls as if radiating outward until it makes its way down to your solar plexus. Your solar plexus is where your personal power comes from. Remember that at all times you are the one in control. Now, that same golden light—so warm, and so comforting—travels down to your sacral charka before making its way to settle at your root chakra. Imagine that golden light forming into a cord, a cord that grounds you to the earth. That grounds you to this life, in this time period. Do you feel it, Jenny?"

Jenny did feel it. She felt the odd sensation that she was connected—but to what she didn't know. So, unsure she simply replied, "Yes."

"Excellent. Now. I am going to use my voice to guide you. When I reach to the number ten, you will have reached your destination. One, imagine that you are at the top of a set of stairs. See the stairs, feel them beneath your feet. Two, you take a step down. Three, you take another step. One foot after the other. Four. You are unsure where the steps lead, but you know that they will lead you somewhere wonderful. Five. Your heart pounds with anticipation as you take another step down. Six. Then another. Seven. You know that you are nearing the bottom. Eight. Your feet find another step and you are so close that you begin to hear the sounds of what awaits at the bottom of the steps. Nine. You can barely contain yourself as you reach the bottom of the steps. Ten."

Jenny's heart pounded in time to Meara's words. But she couldn't quite remember who Meara was. A friend? The voice seemed far away, the memory of who she was even farther. Her feet found the bottom of the cobblestone steps that somehow were etched into her mind. Was she dreaming? She didn't feel as though she were dreaming. In fact, she felt quite awake, more awake than she'd ever felt before. As if her entire body was buzzing at some sort of high frequency. It was as though she could feel, hear, and see all at once. She wasn't here nor there. She simply *was.* Whatever that meant.

The soft voice drifted down to her from the top of the stairs. "Now. Open your eyes. Tell me, what do you see?"

Not one to disobey, Jenny opened her eyes. The light was blinding and at first all she could see was white. Instinctively, her hands flung to her face to protect herself from the jarring brightness.

"Nothing. It's just white. Very, very bright white light." Her own voice sounded far away, as if it were floating up and away from her like a balloon on a summer day.

The other voice drifted down to her again. "It's alright. Give it a minute. Remember what I said about imagination. Often what we imagine is what exists in some other time and in some other place."

That answer made sense. She wondered if she were talking to God. The memory scratched at the corners of her mind, but it seemed fuzzy. No, not God. But who? Maybe it was her own intuition talking. Or a guardian angel. Did it matter?

She noticed that her hands weren't smooth, but had callouses on them. An antiseptic smell filled her nostrils. And something else. The faint smell of…some kind of smoke…and something she couldn't quite place her finger on. Her feet felt crammed into stiff shoes. She could hear the bustle of people around her. Soft voices called out to one another, low, almost-animalistic groans. Squeaky wheels sounded like nails on a chalkboard. But the smell. She couldn't get over the smell. And then it hit her with a wave of nausea. Sickness. Death.

There was a loud crashing sound and the floor beneath her shook, causing her to uncover her eyes and peer around her alarmed. She was in some sort of hospital. Before her were rows of beds, their occupants wrapped and swaddled. Several nurses tended to the patients in the beds. They were all wearing starch white, knee-length dresses, and small caps over their carefully, coifed hair. One of the nurses gave her a strange look as she passed by carrying a tray with various sterilized tools arranged carefully across it.  The lighting was dim and Jenny noticed a string of lightbulbs hanging from the ceiling, but before she could have time to figure it out, that voice whispered softly down to her again.

"Jenny, what do you see?"

"I-I'm in a hospital. Only it's not now. I mean, I'm not sure when it is." She looked around carefully for a sign. Peering down at her own clothing, she noticed that she was wearing the same starched white dress as the other nurses. The shoes she wore were also white and low heeled and she had on stockings. Her fingers found their way from her face to the top of her head, where a small nurse's hat sat perched in her hair. Over the dress was an equally starched white apron. Instinctively, she smoothed her hands across it and noticed the shiny gold wedding band on her left ring finger. Indeed, where and when was she? Who was she married to?

There was another loud crash, and the floor reverberated, fluid bags swayed back and forth beside their patients. Without thinking Jenny put up a hand to stop one from swaying. That's when she noticed the white band with a red cross strapped to her bicep. It had the words: *Deutsche Rotes Kreuz* around it. German Red Cross.

*"Nun, nicht einfach dort stehen. Bewegung*!" Jenny turned at the sound of the voice telling her to not just stand there, but get moving. A blonde-haired woman wearing an identical nurse's uniform to her own strode toward her. Even though the language was harsh and guttural sounding her face was soft. She paused, elbow to eblow with Jenny. Despite the medicinal smell, Jenny got the soft scent of roses and soap. "Do not worry, Adala. Krischen will be fine. He is strong, but more importantly he is smart. If anyone can survive the war, it is your Krischen. You mustn't let your mind wander." Her blue eyes drifted toward the windows of what Jenny now realized was a church. The night was alight with what appeared to be fireworks. "*Schon gut*. Now, there is much work to be done."

Jenny nodded, looking at hospital beds—not an empty one in sight. There was much work to be done. The woman patted her on the shoulder and then continued on her way. It was then Jenny realized the woman had called her Adala. Who was Adala and who was this Krischen the woman spoke of? Why was he fighting in some war? More peculiar, how had Jenny understood the language the nurse had spoken? It was a grating, clipped language that Jenny could recall hearing before. She racked her brain.

Well, duh. If she could read German, then obviously she could understand German too. Maybe she could even speak it herself now. Jenny glanced down at the patient before her, the one whose bed was next to the intravenous fluid stand she had stopped from swaying back and forth after the earth shattering blast. Next to the bed was a chair, over which was draped an olive-colored jacket. Sewn to the jacket's sleeve was an insignia: a bird with open wings and clutched in its talon was a symbol that made a shiver run down Jenny's spine. A symbol she equated to an ideology of hate. A swastika.

She was in Germany, and it was World War II.

# Chapter Four

Jenny didn't have time to think much about it. There were patients in need of care and she was a nurse. Somehow she instinctively knew what to do. She knew where all the supplies were kept, knew how to insert the needle and draw the sample of blood, how to set up the intravenous fluids. She didn't know how she knew, nor did she question it. The skin she was in felt comfortable, familiar, as if she'd come home to an old friend.

She carried a tray of old, dirty bandages to throw into the hazardous waste bin. Not surprisingly, she knew how to change the dressings of the soldiers' wounds. How to cut off the bandages and cleanse the wound in such a way that caused the least amount of discomfort to her patients. She snapped off her latex gloves and dropped them into the same bin as the bandages before heading over to the small wash basin where she rubbed the disinfecting soap over her calloused hands. Glancing up, she caught her reflection in the small mirror above the sink.

Her eyes were still the familiar golden-brown, but her long brown hair was now pinned up in blonde curls. Her face had a spattering of freckles, and her lips were thin and wide. The slight creases that usually graced the outside corner of her eyes were gone, and smooth, young skin peered back at her. She was probably in her early twenties. If that. Her forehead was quite large and she noticed that her eyebrows arched slightly in a way that made her appear startled—or worried. Perhaps she was worried. She rinsed the soap from her fingers, patted her hands dry, then rubbed her thumb against the solid gold of the wedding band. Krischen. *Who was he?*

*"Ah, junge liebe."* Jenny turned. It was the blonde nurse from earlier. "It's late and your shift is nearly over, Adala. Why don't you rest? Go and dream of the return of your sweet Krischen."

"Do you think he'll be back soon?" Jenny found herself asking. It struck her as a silly question considering she didn't even know who he was. But her heart somehow knew and she was sure she could feel it deep in her bones.

"Between you and me," she lowered her voice conspiratorially, "the French and the English will arrive soon and there will be an end to this madness. Now, go Adala. You appear dead on your feet and a tired nurse is of no use to her patients."

Jenny nodded. "Thank you..." And the name escaped her lips without a second thought. "Myna."

The older woman smiled and disappeared back out the door of the small washroom. Jenny's feet led her where she needed to go, stopping at a wooden door with a white sign and a red cross like the one she wore on her armband. She tried the brass knob and the door swung open with a soft groan. Behind the door was a large room. The room was lined with beds and there were makeshift partitions around each one, even though all the nurses were women, there were still medics and doctors who were males. A few nurses were asleep in their beds, snoring softly.

Jenny's aching feet led her to the third bed on the left. A couple of muslin sheets were draped over a clothesline. She gently moved one aside and entered into the small, sacred space that was hers—and hers alone—in this strange world she had fallen into. Suddenly, she felt heavy and leaden with the weight of sleep. Without bothering to change into a clean uniform she all but collapsed into the bed before her, kicking off her shoes so that they hit the floor with a satisfying thud.

She stared at the stone ceiling for a moment before rolling onto her side, placing her hands beneath her cheek. The soapy smell comforted her. She noticed a small table beside the bed with a worn Bible. She reached over and pulled it toward her and as she did so a photograph fell out onto the bed beside her. Before she even looked at it, she knew who it would be of: the mysterious Krischen. She held the photograph carefully between her fingers, as if the faded memory of Krischen would continue to slip away.

A handsome man around her age smiled toward the camera. It was a military photo and Krischen was in full dress regalia. The smile was wide and toothy, but didn't reach his eyes. The photograph was not in color, but she could tell that both Krischen's eyes and hair were dark. He was broad shouldered and had angular cheekbones that made him appear very serious. She turned the photograph over and in a sloppy, scrawling handwriting were the words: *meine liebe, mein licht.* My love, my light. Jenny smiled. The words comforted her.

She set the Bible back on the small table, and then closed her eyes, resting the photograph on her chest.

Jenny—Adala—knew, deep down that she was here, in this place—a small church in Germany amidst World War II, witnessing firsthand perhaps the single most horrific thing in the history of humanity. She knew too that she was married to this man, Krischen, and that he was fighting with the *Wehermacht*, even though they both knew, as good Christians do, that all are equal in the eyes of God. And that God was always watching. Yet. At the same time, she had a nagging sense that she was somewhere else too. Far away, maybe even in another time or place. Somewhere else, where she was not Adala, not a nurse. And not married to Krischen. She shivered. A place without Krischen is not one where she wanted to be.

She raised her knuckle to her lips and kissed the golden ring before her eyelids slid closed, finally succumbing to fatigue.

*Nach hause kommen, mein Leiebe.*

Come home, my Love.

*Eile.*

Hurry.

## Chapter Five

The nap was short-lived as there was a commotion. Adala sat up quickly listening to the hushed voices of the nurses.

"The Commander is here!"

"But why?" came the whined reply from another nurse, her voice still drowsy with sleep. "There is no reason. The soldiers are well-taken care of."

Adala stood up quietly and peered between the muslin sheets at the two women talking. The photograph of Krischen laid on the still-made bed, so tired she hadn't even bothered to turn down the blankets. One of the nurses had chestnut brown hair that was in a loose ponytail. Her face was creased with worry. The other nurse—the one with the whiny voice—had jet black hair that was pinned up beneath her nurse's cap. The black-haired nurse appeared young, even younger than Adala. Almost a child. She thought for a moment. Perhaps she was a child.

The older woman's reply was curt. "Daughter, you know why."

The young nurse's dark eyes widened. "No."

Her mother reached up pulling something off her neck and dropping it into the pocket of her nurse's apron. "That will be enough. I told you to trust no one. But you never do listen."

"I didn't tell anyone," the girl whispered, but it sounded more like a comfort to herself than to her mother.

The older nurse's tone softened. "There are eyes and ears everywhere, my little lamb." She sighed. "Besides it was only a matter of time."

"We can hide." The girl's voice was frightened. *Was she even really a nurse?* Adala found herself wondering. She tried to quickly put the pieces together. The two women were clearly mother and daughter. And they feared the Commander, which could only mean—they were Jewish. A cold dagger sliced through Adala's heart.

"No. We will face our fate like proud Jews. We

will not embarrass our brethren," the mother scolded.

Without thought, Adala burst through the curtain. The girl's hand flew to her mouth in surprise. "Adala, how long have you been hiding there?"

Adala tried to smile, but the panic deep within her pulled at the corners of her mouth and it came out as a frown. "Your necklace. Here." She put her hands to her own neck, knowing it was there but somehow noticing it for the first time, the silver cross that hung there. She undid the clasp with shaking fingers and without permission, began to fasten it around the neck of the young girl. "Today, Keren, you are not a Jew. At least for this moment." The name came to her memory easily.

"Adala…" The older woman began to protest.

"The necklace." Adala held out her palm, directed toward Keren's mother…Sharon. Sharon was her name. "Sharon, the necklace." They could hear footsteps hurrying down the hallway. The Head Nurse was coming to summon them to the patient ward. "Please." It came out more of a command than a platitude.

Sharon sighed, reaching into her pocket and dropping the necklace in Adala's waiting palm. "You are a fool."

"Perhaps I am a fool. But the Lord is always

watching and I will do right by my Savior." The words seemed too eloquent for Adala—at least for who Adala thought she was.

Another nurse burst into the room, breathless. "The Commander. Come. *Schnell.*" Then she disappeared back down the hallway.

Adala, Keren, and Sharon exchanged uneasy glances. For a moment time seemed to stand still as Keren and Sharon joined hands, then each reached for Adala's hand, whispering a Hebrew prayer of encouragement, before exiting the sleeping quarters.

∞

The Commander walked stiffly, his medals of honor glowing in the dim light of the makeshift patient ward, his boot heels clicking across the stone floor. The nurses were lined up shoulder to shoulder down the center row, patient beds along either side. He glowered at the line of nurses. "I have heard that this hospital harbors Jews."

The Head Nurse spoke up softly. "Surely, Commander, you do not question the loyalty of those who keep your soldiers healthy and alive?"

The Commander's eyes were narrow in his face, like a bald eagle about to swoop down and devour its prey, but not before first engaging it in a little cat-and-mouse. Adala had her shoulders back, her chin jutted out proudly, but her heart pounded loudly in her chest. Sharon was to her left and Keren to her right. "I would like to see the papers for all of your nurses stationed here, *Oberpfleger."* The Head Nurse's blue eyes flinched, but she turned on her heel and walked away, presumably to fetch the papers.

A young Captain stepped forward from behind the Commander. He was probably not much older than Adala. "All the women with dark hair and dark eyes please line up to the left. All the women with light-colored hair and eyes, please line up to the right."

There was a low murmur of protest from the nurses, but they began to jostle about obeying the orders. It didn't make any sense. Surely, anyone with a sense of logic, knew that anyone could be a Christian or Jew regardless of hair or eye color, didn't they? Adala stood in the middle, squished between the two lines. Her hair was blonde, but her eyes were a golden-brown. She was unsure of which line she should stand in. Finally, she decided to stay in the line with Sharon and Keren. Her hand found its way into the pocket of her nurse's apron, still dirty from earlier when she hadn't changed before falling asleep. Keren's Star of David was nestled deep in its corner, but what did it matter if the Commander has asked for their papers? Adala knew what that meant. Papers were lineage. It was a death sentence waiting to happen. But maybe, Keren and Sharon were smart enough to lie if they had gotten this far already.

The Head Nurse returned with a folder which she presented to the Commander. She bit her lip and then fell into line with the light-haired, blue-eyed nurses. The Commander ruffled through the papers, looking at each paper and then tossing it to the floor. They seemed to flutter in slow motion, like petals dropping from a flower.

"These are all of the papers, *Fraulein*?" His voice was an angry bark.

"It appears so." Her reply was curt. She protected her own. "Now, if you are finished. We have patients to which we need to attend." She held her chin up defiantly, daring the Commander to question her. His beak of a nose was inches from hers and Adala found that she was holding her breath.

The Commander tossed the folder onto the floor, his boots crunching over the papers—the lineage of each nurse—as if they were leaves on a fall day. Maybe it was a fall day. Adala had seemed to lose all sense of time in this place. The Commander strode between the two lines of women, the Captain close at his heels like a well-behaved lap dog.

Reaching Keren he paused and Adala could hear the intake of breath behind her, but instead he stepped beside Adala, his pale fingers finding her chin and turning it toward him. "My, what beautiful eyes you have." His fingers were cold and his gaze was hungry.

Adala stared at him. "I am a married woman, Commander. My husband fights in your war."

His grin was like that of a wolf before devouring a succulent pig. "That has never stopped me before." He dropped his hand back to his side and turned back toward the Head Nurse. "Two days, *Fraulein*. If you do not produce what I am looking for, then this one will do."

## *Chapter Six*

She had to run. Even if it meant Krischen would have a harder time finding her. In her eyes, there was no choice to be had. Throughout her shift, Adala's mind raced with thoughts. *How would she escape unseen? Where would she go*? The bombings seemed the worst at night, so it was probably best if she left in the wee hours before sunrise. The darkness was the best time to remain hidden.

Her hands moved without the instruction of her mind. She moved fluidly from patient to patient, checking their vital signs and making notes, and replenishing intravenous fluids. The hours of her shift flew by because there was always something needing to be done.

It was nearing the end of her rounds, and there was one more patient in need of her attention—Patient

Nineteen. He'd been badly wounded and it was routine to change his bandages regularly to prevent infection. Adala set to work, methodically undressing his various wounds in order to administer some topical ointments. She worked quickly. His eyes were closed, but his eyelids fluttered as if he were dreaming. Regardless, she continued her work, as quietly and as gently as possible so as not to draw attention. She knew that the soldiers had nightmares and sometimes if they woke up caught in the middle, it took them several moments to realize where they were. Pouring some alcohol into a gauze pad she held her breath and murmured a silent prayer before pressing it to the gaping wound in his leg. The prayer wasn't enough.

Patient Nineteen's eyes flung open. She tried to pull away but instinctively he grabbed her wrist, his fingers digging into her flesh. Surprisingly strong for someone wounded. "Please," she whispered trying to hold back the tears and remain calm. "Let me help you. I am a nurse. I am here. You are here."

The man blinked. He was about her age with sandy colored hair and dark stubble across his chin. His blue eyes went from unseeing to cognizant and when they landed on her face they softened. He loosened his grip, but didn't let go and Adala's hand still hovered between them the gauze pad clutched between her fingers.

"I am here," he said. The words came out garbled, like his mouth was full of cotton. He cleared his throat. "I am here."

"Yes. You—we—are here." Adala recalled how in her training she was taught to talk to the soldiers in calm, soothing tones and in severe circumstances to not try and rationalize with them. Between the war and any medications they could be taking, their moments of lucidity could be short and few. But when this solider looked at her his blue eyes were as clear as the sky at sunrise.

"Where is here again?" he asked her still not letting go of her wrist. He needed her at that moment, only she didn't realize it. He needed to feel tethered to the spot, to reality, because if he didn't find an anchor surely he would float away back into his nightmares and never return.

"The hospital. In the Church of the Holy Angels."

The solider had deep, dark circles beneath his eyes and a faded scar that ran across his left cheek. He smiled. "That's ironic."

"How so?" Adala asked before she could stop

herself. *Don't try to rationalize with them.*

"Well, at first I thought I was dead and that you were an angel. But then I saw your face and your nurse's uniform and remembered that it was the war. It is ironic to me that I would be in a place of angels while the mayhem of hell rained down around us. *Then the devil left him, and behold, angels came and were ministering to him."*

"I am no angel, I assure you."

His smile widened. "You are kind and you tend to my wounds. Could have fooled me."

"It is my duty."

"Being kind isn't a duty." This time Adala smiled and the man let go of her wrist. She looked down and there were red marks where his fingers had gripped her so tightly. He noticed. "Sorry about that."

"You were confused." She looked down at the gauze pad in her hand, still damp with the alcohol. "May I?"

He nodded and closed his eyes. She heard the sharp intake of breath and she moved as quickly as she could, cleansing the wound then redressing it in clean bandages. When she was finished he opened one eye.

"What's your name?" His eye sparkled, not dull like the other heavily medicated patients.

"I'm a married woman." She replied, but nonetheless the flush still crept up to her cheeks.

"So? You're married. You can't tell someone your name if you are married? Is that some sort of law I didn't know about?" He was teasing. What did it matter that he had asked her name? It was only a name.

"Adala." For some reason the words tumbled out of her mouth. "It means noble one."

"That's a beautiful name. And considering I thought you were an angel for a minute there, an apt one as well."

She began to clean up the soiled bandages, placing them in a small bucket with the others. "What about you? What's your name?"

"Can you not see it in your papers?"

She shook her head. "Nope. You are just listed as Patient Nineteen."

This time he shook his head, a lock of hair falling across his forehead. "So impersonal! Serving one's country in the grandest war the world has seen, and reduced to nothing but a number."

Adala clucked disapprovingly. "It's how we keep track of the patients. The higher the number, the more recently the patient arrived. It works for our record-keeping purposes. Besides most of the patients aren't lucid enough for a conversation."

"But a name—a name is so important!" he protested. "It is like a badge that we wear, a label telling the world exactly who we are! We only get one name."

"Is that so? Then what, pray tell, is the label you wear?" Adala didn't know why she was engaging with Patient Nineteen in this absurd game, in the middle of the night, while the other patients lay asleep all around them. In the distance she could hear the thunderous cry of the bombs being dropped across the landscape, but in this moment she found a simple pleasure in their conversation.

"Well, Adala." Her name rolled off his tongue easily, as if it were familiar to him and as though he'd said it many times before. "You can call me Evert. Unless, of course, you'd still like to refer to me as Patient Nineteen, for record-keeping's sake." His grin was playful.

This time Adala smiled back. "Evert will do."

# Chapter Seven

Adala should have left. But she didn't. It would only be a matter of time before the Commander returned. She should have ignored Evert's attempts to engage her in conversation, when the rest of the hospital was quiet and asleep, their voices hushed whispers. But she didn't. She was right. He wasn't much older than she—only a couple of years. Before the mandatory military service, he was studying to be a doctor at one of the more prestigious German universities. He was the only son in a family with three girls. Adala listened as he described different adventures from his childhood to her: the family's trip to Sweden where he went skiing for the first time and broke his leg, his eldest sister passing from tuberculosis when he was only ten fueling his ambition to study medicine, and many more.

She found herself hurrying through her rounds in order to pull up a chair beside Evert's bed and listen to his tales. He was a wonderful storyteller—descriptive and elaborate, pausing at all the right places to ensure the most suspense. He revealed the scar across his cheek was from a bar fight over the love of his life. "Well," he admitted sheepishly, "the love of my life at the time." Adala had laughed at this, having to stifle the raucous sound with her knuckles in order to not wake the sleeping hospital.

During the day she would sleep and she found herself dreaming of Evert—not Krischen. The dreams didn't make sense really, but that's the nature of dreams she rationalized. She dreamt they were skiing together on a beautiful, bright day. Everything was crisp and brilliant, as if it were in some sort of hyper-focus. She could even smell the freshly fallen snow and the deep, clean scent of pine. The sun was warm on her cheeks. In reality, she'd never even been skiing before. But she'd never had a dream that felt more real.

Slowly, thoughts of Krischen began to subside. Somehow, it seemed like another lifetime and memories of her husband—only married for three months before called to service—began to fade like the photograph that sat tucked inside her Bible. Sharon commented that she seemed different—sharper and healthier. Adala shrugged it off, but one morning, prior to the end of her shift and the start of Keren's, the younger nurse pulled her aside.

"It's that soldier, isn't it?" she'd asked in an excited whisper. The fear from the incident with the Commander—their near capture—replaced with a newer self-assurance, at least for now.

"I don't know what you're talking about," Adala had murmured as she headed toward her muslin partition. Undeterred, Keren followed her.

"Patient Nineteen."

"He's just a lonely man who is far away from his family."

"I bet you know his name." She was persistent, Adala would give her that.

"What matter is it if I know his name? We all have names. We should be called as such. Only the Nazis refer to people as numbers."

Keren was silent for a beat, but having decided to ignore Adala's comment, she refuted. "Names mean attachment. Think about if you go to buy a puppy. A puppy is a puppy is a puppy," she smiled knowingly. "Until you name it."

"Evert is not a puppy. He's a man."

"I knew it!" Keren practically squealed with delight.

"I'm a married woman." Adala said, but it was more a reminder to herself than to Keren. Yet, the words felt foreign as they left her lips.

"Married in head maybe, but not in heart." Adala turned her back to Keren to change out of her uniform. She heard the younger nurse's footsteps grow softer as she departed for the patient ward.

Was it true? She hadn't known Krischen long before marrying him. They'd met through a mutual friend, only knowing one another a month, before getting married. The war somehow seemed to expedite things—hurrying them along as if time was somehow simultaneously slowing and quickening at the same time. The horrors dragged on, but time also seemed to be running out. She thought she was in love with Krischen, but after meeting and talking to Evert she realized how little she really knew about him. She couldn't recall how many sisters or brothers he had. Was it two sisters and one brother? Or the other way around? Had he ever had a family vacation? Broken any bones? These were all things she didn't know about him. They were things he didn't even know about her either.

She sat on the bed, her mind spinning. She kicked off her shoes. Surely, if he'd ever taken a family vacation wasn't all that important, yet in this moment it seemed vital that she should know. She swung her legs up onto the bed and rested her head back on the fluffed pillow behind her. As she reached for the lamp near the bed, her gold ring glinted in the dimness. It made her stomach lurch and suddenly she felt as if the very thing would burn a mark into her skin. She slipped it off and somehow it felt as if a great weight had been lifted from her shoulders. She pulled her Bible toward her, opened it to a random page, and placed the ring inside before shutting it and placing it back on the nightstand. Who she had thought she was before the war, was no longer who she believed herself to be. The world would be different when the war was over. Forgiveness would be needed. Her own private world would be no exception.

∞

One evening as Adala tended to Evert's wounds, which were healing up nicely much to her chagrin—she feared he'd heal much too quickly and be turned back into service—he surprised her when she leaned in close.

"Let's run away." His voice was low and throaty. He sounded…serious.

She tried to discredit his words, shooing them away with a wave of her hand as she dropped the dirty bandages into the bucket. "To where?"

His lips smiled, but his eyes were solemn. "Anywhere." He gestured. "Pick a place."

She decided to play along, pulling the chair up beside his bed, so close that her elbow brushed against his. She snapped off her gloves and dropped them into the pail with the bandages. "Australia?"

Evert shook his head. "Too exotic."

"China?"

He shook his head again. "Too many people."

"America." This time it didn't come out a question. He turned to her, blue eyes thoughtful.

"Yes. Let's go to America."

"How? There is a war going on. We cannot just up and leave." Her words protested, but her heart began to pound in her chest. The patient ward was quiet, only disrupted by the occasional outbursts of one of the newer patients. An older man who Adala would leave Evert's side to tend to. He had very bad nightmares and sometimes required the strength of multiple nurses to calm him down.

Evert took up the conversation as soon as she returned to his side. "But can't we? You're but one of hundreds of nurses and I'm a wounded soldier. No one will miss us." There was a subtle excitement to his voice. Adala had grown used to the tales of his childhood, the familiarity of the way they verbally sparred back and forth. She'd grown accustomed to his wounds and scars, both the ones she tended to on his body and the ones he periodically revealed in his heart. "What will you do if he returns?"

At first she thought he was referring to the Commander, but then she remembered that he wasn't cognizant yet when that happened. It was over two weeks ago now that the Commander had visited. Somehow it felt longer. She realized he meant Krischen. He had noticed she no longer wore the ring; she had told him the story. Two people—practically strangers—caught up in the romance of war, only now she knew war was not romantic. It was heart-wrenching, violent, and frightening. Krischen killed men and she was the one who tried to save them. She had been naïve.

"He may not return."

Evert shook his head. "But he may." He turned his head so the unscarred cheek faced her. "If I knew I was coming home to you, I'd do everything in my power to stay alive. Heck, just that would be enough to keep me alive." There was a long pause. "I think it's what brought me back to life here right now."

"You thought I was an angel." He turned back toward her and picked up her hand. His hands were calloused like hers. Before he began to study medicine he had been a masonry apprentice, because his father was a mason, before realizing it wasn't his passion. *We only get one life,* he'd told her. *It is our responsibility to follow our passion.*

"You are an angel." His voice was low and raspy again. She leaned in closer to hear him. He touched her face, his hand practically encompassing her entire cheek. In one grand gesture, he pulled her toward him, taking in her soapy, lightly floral scent. His unshaven cheek was rough against her skin as he moved his lips toward hers and kissed her deeply. He'd been wanting to do that, but wasn't sure she'd accept his advances, but much to his delight she kissed him back. It was passion, but it was something more. It was like a deep knowing of two lives intertwined, as if everything they'd experienced in their separate lives was vital to them arriving at this exact moment in time together.

Adala pulled away, her chin resting on Evert's chest, her hand still wrapped inside his. "I think," she whispered, "that I'd very much like America."

# Chapter Eight

The plan was that they'd leave immediately after Adala's nightly round in one week's time. There were usually two doctors at any given time overseeing the hospital, not to mention the clergy who still resided in other parts of the church. Meaning, cars would be available. Adala didn't know how to drive—it just wasn't something a woman needed to know in 1943. But Evert assured her he knew how if only she could secure a set of keys. His leg wound was practically healed and Adala was confident if they could minimize the amount of walking, Evert would be just fine. Adala would rest her chin on Evert's chest as they murmured into the wee hours of the morning about their plans and the life they would build once they arrived in America.

In the days leading up to their departure, Adala had taken small rations of medical supplies: a pack of gauze here, a roll of bandages there, knowing that the inventory was done weekly and would be conducted after they were gone. At dinner she saved tiny scraps of food—mainly the things that wouldn't spoil—in the hopes that it would help them until they got to the next place. Wherever that was.

Unfortunately, not everything could be planned and accounted for. Such as the return of the Commander. It was the last day before her evening shift—her last rounds as a nurse—before her and Evert were supposed to leave. The nurses stood single file in between the hospital beds as the Commander and his SS soldiers conducted searches, checking the records the Head Nurse had handed to him upon his request. He glanced at the papers as he walked down the line of nurses, eagle eyes calculating. His boot heels clicked along the stone floor, echoing against the high ceilings in the silence of the space. As he neared her, Adala found that she was holding her breath. At last he reached her.

"Ah," he said glancing down at the papers in his hand and back down to Adala. Her heart pounded in her chest and she could feel sweat drip along her spine and down to her tailbone. "Adala. A beautiful name."

Her voice came out small. "Thank you, Sir."

"It says here you are of German descent."

"That is correct."

"And do you enjoy being a nurse?" The question wasn't all that strange, she was used to the pleasantries of the various authorities that came in and out of the hospital.

"I enjoy helping people, Sir."

"That's admirable." He reached out a hand as if he were going to straighten her nurse's cap, when something seemed to catch his eye. She felt the color drain from her face. He had noticed something. Something was out of place. Sure, her own previous night's shift had only just finished a few hours ago, she'd barely had any sleep, giddy with excitement over the forthcoming chapter of her life, only to be awoken early because the Commander had arrived.

His hand lingered by her face. He smelled of cigarette smoke and whiskey. The smell made her stomach roil. She wanted to flinch away, but knew that it would not be in her best interest. He reached toward the cuffed sleeve of her uniform. She held her breath. He pulled out a necklace, a delicate gold chain. From the end hung the Star of David. Keren's necklace! She had forgotten to take it out of her apron pocket all those weeks ago. Somehow, in the wash bins, it must have fallen out of the pocket and gotten stuck in the cuff of her nurse's uniform.

An angry look clouded the Commander's face, creasing his forehead and making him seem much older. "You carry the symbol of a Jew?" He dropped the dainty chain to the floor and ground the heel of his boot over it, grinding it into the stone.

Before she could speak, another nurse thrust herself out of the line. Landing on her knees. "Please! It was mine!" Keren.

The Commander turned, noticing the young woman, but not the look of horror that one of the other nurse's wore on her own face. Sharon. "Grab her!"

"No!" The words came flying out of Adala's mouth before she could stop them. "She's a fool! It is my necklace."

"Your papers say you are a Christian German."

The lie came out smoothly. "I am. But I married a Jew. Check the Bible by my bed station. Inside you will find a ring engraved with the words *My Love My Light,* a reference to Psalm 27:1 in which David—King of the

Israelites claims his love of the Lord."

The Commander did not turn. "Check her belongings."

Keren stifled her tears as Sharon pulled her back to her feet and into the nurse's line. She hung her head as she cried softly.

Time seemed to stretch and expand as the SS soldier searched for Adala's belongings. He returned with the Bible under his arm, and holding the golden wedding band over his head as if in victory. "The Jew lover's words are true, Commander! Here is the ring to prove it."

The Commander turned and slapped Adala across the cheek. He spit at her feet, then shoved her in the direction of the soldiers, who grabbed her by either arm. She didn't have time to process the sting in her cheek because she was too busy realizing what she had just done—so instinctively. It was true: she enjoyed helping people.

He turned to the Head Nurse. "And you—you are lucky we don't take you for harboring a Jew sympathizer."

The Head Nurse showed no emotion. "And how am I to know who these women marry? I am not their pastor, I am their Head Nurse. They do their jobs and I have no complaints."

The soldiers' grip tightened on her arms and they began to pull her toward the church doors. Her legs felt like jelly and her head felt numb. There was the sound of something being knocked over and a tall man—well over six feet tall—came barreling down the aisle with a chair held high over his head. And it was the first time that she had seen him standing. He looked strong and mighty.

Evert swung the chair with one hand as he came down the aisle, but it only proved to be a distraction as he reached into his patient gown and a gunshot rang out, causing the nurses to scatter for cover. The soldiers loosened their grip on Adala's arms and everything seemed to happen in slow motion.

"My Love!" Adala cried out and it came out strangled and alien sounding. The Commander had a dark stain forming on his left shoulder.

"Run!" Evert called out, a gun aimed surely at the soldiers on her either side, but she felt frozen to the spot.

The soldiers pulled out their guns. There were loud shots and Evert crumbled to the floor. Adala ran to him and this time no one tried to stop her. She slid across the floor, smearing his blood as she scooped him up into her arms. She cradled his head like a small child in her arms.

"Get out!" The Head Nurse was screaming at the soldiers.

Evert tried to smile up at her, but instead blood spilled out from between his lips.

"*Shh.*" Adala whispered.

"You...are...a...noble...woman." The tears streamed down her face at his words. She didn't feel like a noble woman. Right now she felt more like a broken one.

"We're going to America," she whispered to him, rocking back and forth. "We're going to get married and have a family. You'll be a doctor and I'll be...I'll be..." His eyes went blank before she could get out the rest of the words. His chest stilled.

More soldiers came rushing in. Nurses scrambled to get supplies. Clergy came running from other parts of the church. But none of it mattered now. It didn't matter that Krischen might die in the name of this war or that she would most likely die because of her actions. But Keren wouldn't die. She was so young, only a child, and after the war she would go and live her life. Maybe she would even go to America and get married. Have a family of her own.

The soldiers gripped her shoulders, but she refused to let go of Evert. She let out an animalistic howl and only when the soldiers let her shoulders go did she press her cheek to that of her true love.

War brought out both the worst and somehow the best of humanity.

Adala wept.

# Chapter Nine

Jenny felt the sensation that she was crying. The pain Adala felt was so real. Adala's pain was in fact her pain. She had been there. She had lived that life. Maybe even was still living that life in some sort of twisted, mixed-up sense of time and space.

"Evert was right," Meara said quietly. "Adala, was very noble."

"It's not just that," Jenny found herself saying, except it wasn't herself. It was a faraway version of herself. Not Adala, but also not Jenny. A version of both of them that was both older and wiser. "In Hebrew, the name means *justice*. Adala's life was a personal statement in a time of great injustice."

"Are any of the people from Adala's life part of the same Oversoul?" Meara asked. Jenny didn't know what an Oversoul was, but she found herself answering anyway.

"Indeed. Evert, is of course, part of the same Oversoul. As are Keren and the Commander."

"Not Krischen?"

"No, not Krischen."

"Do you wish to explain to Jenny what the Oversoul is?" Meara asked. Jenny could hear her scribbling in a notebook.

"An Oversoul is a larger soul. We all emanate from the same place and we all wish to be as omniscient as the Universe—or God or Life Force—therefore it is more efficient for a soul to fracture into numerous counterparts in order to learn and extract life lessons more quickly." Jenny knew this answer didn't come from her, in fact she had never even heard of an Oversoul, and yet at the same time she had the deep sense that she had somehow known it all along. Similar to how a baby upon birth has the primal instinct of breath.

"What lessons is Jenny to extract from the life of Adala?" Meara asked. Her voice was calm and even. But also inquisitive.

"Humanity."

"Humanity? Treating others with kindness and compassion?" Meara prompted.

"Not only that. More simply, what it means to be human. Period," Jenny replied. "To be human is to be both light and dark. Without the one we cannot have the other. If the Commander had not shown the dark, Adala may not have stepped forward to reveal the light."

"I see. In these bodies we are limited only to our thoughts, feelings, and actions. Other souls also having a life experience provide the contrast."

"Yes, contrast is a lovely word. Human beings are full of contrast."

"Anything else that Jenny should be aware of?" Meara prompted.

"Only that Adala's actions were not in vain. Not only did our soul learn an important lesson about humanity, but Keren never forgot the sacrifice of neither her friend nor of Evert. Because of that Keren led quite a miraculous life, becoming a Jewish Historian after immigrating to America with her fiancé after the war. They had a large family and lived well into an old age."

"That's reassuring. I'm sure Adala would be pleased to know that."

"Human existence is fleeting. Even in the throes of darkness the light of hope still shines like a beacon. It's yet another important lesson that our time here has revealed to us."

"Are there more lessons for Jenny to observe?"

"Yes, many."

"Shall we continue another day then?" Meara asked.

"It would be best," came the response.

"Okay then. Jenny, I will guide you back up to the present. I will count down from ten and with each number you will become more aware of your present life and your current surroundings. Ten, you are leaving your other life behind. Nine, it is fading. Eight, growing fainter as if you are floating away. Seven, the light of the past is growing dimmer. And now, six, you see the light of the present in front of you start as a pinprick. Five. The pinprick grows brighter. Four and you feel yourself being pulled toward it. Three, it begins to encompass you. You feel lighter as you become aware. Two, of what it feels like to be back inside your current body. Back to the present. One. Open your eyes, Jenny. Welcome back."

# Chapter Ten

Jenny took a sip of warm lemon water. Meara insisted that it would help her feel grounded. They were sitting back in the reception area.

"So an Oversoul is like, what? One giant soul that splinters off into tinier fragments?"

"Something like that," Meara tapped her pen on top of her notepad thoughtfully. "It's the soul's way of being more efficient. This plane—the Earth plane—was created for us to manifest in human form, to be able to experience physicality. So in order to learn all there is to learn here, the soul separates into multiple bodies. That's where the concept of soulmates comes from, it's a little bit of a misnomer."

Jenny's head was spinning. She could remember Adala, but it was a bit fuzzy. Like she had woken from a dream that was now beginning to fade. Meara had told her if she regressed again that she'd become better at remembering. She still felt like herself and she supposed that was the most important thing. Yet, at the same time she somehow felt lighter as if something heavy she didn't even know she had been carrying was now lifted.

"I recorded the session for you and will send it in a MP4 file to your email. I'll also transcribe my notes for you. I will say you've had one of the more vivid regressions in my database of clients."

"I've always had really vivid dreams...since I was a kid." Jenny held the mug in both hands, drawing in its comforting warmth. The dreams were one of the reasons Hadley had recommended she try the regression in the first place.

"I hope that you'll review the files and call me if you have any questions." She looked thoughtful for a moment. Then gave a slight nod as if she had had a silent discussion with herself. "And call me when you're ready for your next appointment."

"My next appointment?" Jenny had thought this would be her only appointment. How many lives could one person have lived?

"When you're ready. I think you'll find that what your Higher Self had to say was quite intriguing. Plus, with the vividness of your regression…Jenny, you are quite an old soul. And…how do I say this? The lessons your soul is here to learn are ones that could benefit many others on their journeys."

"What are you saying?"

"I'm not saying anything. Yet. But I will tell you that I am writing a book of my clients' experiences, with their permission of course. And I would be honored if you would be willing to continue our sessions, in the hopes that your experiences could help guide others."

*I enjoy helping others, Sir.*

The voice was not hers, but the words were. They felt familiar. But their exact origins remained a bit fuzzy too, like the rest of the regression.

"I'll think about it." Jenny conceded. In general, she was a private person. Sure, she expressed herself through her works of art, but she only had a couple of close friends: Hadley and another friend who lived in Colorado. She had a few acquaintances and even a Facebook account, except she never used it. She couldn't even remember her password anymore.

Meara smiled as if that were the answer that she expected. "Please do." She reached into her pocket and pulled out a sleek cigarette case, but instead of a cigarette she pulled out a business card and handed it to Jenny. The card was a seafoam green with a black filigree border. *Meara Stolarz, PhD. Regression Therapist @ pastlives444@drmearastolarz.com* was written in a simple italicized script. She hadn't realized that Meara had a doctorate degree.

"You're a doctor?" she asked dumbly.

"Well, not a medical one, obviously. But yes, I have a Doctorate in Metaphysical Science. I don't include the title doctor in most things." She gave an embarrassed smile. "I think it's a bit pretentious."

Jenny slipped the card into the pocket of her jean jacket. "You don't think it would help people take you more seriously?"

Meara shrugged. "Other people's opinions of me aren't any of my business." She rose from her chair and Jenny followed her to the door. Before she left, she turned prepared to shake Meara's hand, but instead Meara wrapped an arm around her shoulder in a sort of half hug. "Company policy," she explained as she pulled away.

"Thank you," Jenny said as she stepped back into the hallway.

"You're definitely welcome. See you soon." She said it with utmost confidence before softly shutting the door behind Jenny.

The hallway somehow seemed different. It was the same drab carpet and outdated wall décor and yet it seemed brighter, almost as if she had to squint to see clearly. The elevator was already waiting when she reached it. She stepped inside and pressed the button for the first floor. The doors closed and the elevator began its slow descent, but Jenny—her mind spinning with the afternoon's events—didn't even seem to notice.

∞

Later that evening as she sat on the couch watching *X-Files* reruns with her dog, a mutt rescue named Caddie, her phone buzzed. The little envelope icon indicated that she had an email. She clicked on it, expecting the transcript and audio file from Meara. Instead she did a double take when she saw the name of the message's sender.

Kevin Foley.

# Chapter Eleven

Her heart stopped in her chest. She hadn't talked to Kevin in over a year. What could he want? Jenny's mind immediately went the path of least resistance, the one Hansel and Gretl would have followed into the forest. Maybe he had met someone and is getting married. That would be her luck. As if he being the one to end the relationship wasn't bad enough. Of course, he would find someone before she did.

Jenny grabbed a coffee pod and stuck it into the machine that rested on the countertop. She chewed on her thumbnail while she waited, the earthy aroma filling the small kitchen. Or, she allowed herself the sweet morsel, he wanted to get back together. Sure, it had been a long time, but people changed. And they changed their minds all the time too. Her stomach did a little flip-flop. Is that what she wanted? She reached for the coffee mug and as she did the seafoam-green colored card glared at her from the side of the refrigerator.

As if it weren't causing her enough anxiety already, her phone buzzed from its seat on the couch for a second time. Caddie looked at her lazily—*Well, you answer it. I don't have thumbs.* She flopped onto the couch and picked up her phone. Another email message. Except this time it was the one she had expected the first time. It was from Meara. The subject line simply read: *Audio and Transcript.* At least she, unlike some people, wrote something in the subject line. It was trivial to most people, but one of Jenny's pet peeves, one that Hadley also happened to be guilty of all the time. Jenny loved her friend enough to forgive her, but she was never long to remind her that the subject line was there for a reason.

She took a sip of coffee and pretended to ignore the previous email from Kevin. She wanted to know—quite badly—what it contained. But she also dreaded whatever it may contain. Setting down her coffee she took three steps across the small living space and picked her MacBook off the small desk that was shoved against the wall. Her art studio was located in the second bedroom. She didn't see the point in having a guest room as she didn't have many—okay *any*—guests. This email she wanted to open on the computer so that she could listen to the entire transcript, which she knew would be almost two hours long. Meara's note was short and sweet.

*Jenny,*

*Enclosed you will find your full-length regression audio and its transcript. I hope that you find it both moving and insightful. Again, if you have any questions don't hesitate to contact me.*

*Hope to see you soon,*

*M.*

Jenny right-clicked on the audio button and selected download. While she waited she clicked the transcript and it popped open. She figured she may as well follow along, in case part of the audio was garbled or confusing. In the background from the TV, Mulder was saying something about wanting to believe—needing to believe—and Scully was telling him she'd believe it when the science could back it up. Mulder always worked in leaps of faith. Scully needed concrete proof. But wasn't part of believing having the faith that something could exist—without any science to back it up? Belief didn't come after science. It came before it. *Beliefs are simply repeated thoughts. Nothing more. Nothing less.* Jenny shook her head, muted the TV, and then clicked the play button.

∞

The room was awash in lavender gray light. Jenny woke up with a gasp. Caddie shot her a withering look, but her ears were pert with concern. The room began to come back into focus as Jenny's eyes adjusted. The armoire and matching dresser, the painting of the Carolina shore she'd done some years ago, the picture of her with Hadley on vacation in North Carolina, and her favorite Buddha statue, his belly worn from her superstitious rubbing. It was morning. Well, morning for people who liked to be awake at 6 AM. She rubbed her eyes and noticed her face was damp. She had been crying. Not yet ready to begin the day, she sank back into the pillows which satisfied Caddie who curled back up into a ball, but not before shooting Jenny with another glare at having been disturbed.

Why had she been crying? Often she had very intense dreams and sometimes days, weeks—sometimes even years!—later she could recall them in full Technicolor detail. Then she remembered. Before bed she had begun listening to the transcript of her regression. She'd only meant to listen to a little bit of it, not the full two hours, but she found herself riveted by the story of Adala and her life. A World War II nurse working to save the very lives that could kill her new husband and her friend, Keren, who was a Jew. Once Adala had mentioned Evert, Jenny couldn't stop listening. She'd quit following along in the transcript and sat with her eyes closed as she listened. She knew it was her saying the words, but at the same time it hadn't felt like her. Her, but different.

Now, she knew why she had been crying. She couldn't stop playing the images her mind painted of Evert being shot by the Nazi soldiers. She could see it—could feel it—as if it were her experience, like she herself was there. Her stomach clenched at the memory. It was almost as though she could smell the metallic scent of the shed blood and feel its stickiness on her fingers. And the love Adala felt. It was so deep and vast. She'd loved Krischen—whoever he was—no doubt, but Evert. Evert was her soulmate. She tried to recall what her Higher Self had said to Meara. Something about Keren and the life she went on to live. Maybe that meant Keren is part of the same Oversoul too. Jenny made a mental note to ask Meara about it. Wait. Did that mean she was planning on seeing Meara again? Her heart seemed to say *yes,* but her mind still was saying *no*. Maybe first she'd talk to Hadley about it. Hadley would understand. Besides, it was her idea anyways.

She reached for her phone, ready to dial her best friend, then did a mental head slap. It was 6 AM, unless it was an emergency she'd either wake Hadley up or give her a heart attack. The email notification was still in the task bar, reminding her that Kevin's message still waited. No. She still wasn't ready for that can of worms just yet. At this point there was no way she was going to fall back asleep, so much to Caddie's nerve, she slipped out of bed and into her favorite slippers, dropping a hooded sweatshirt over her head before padding into the next room.

Even though she hadn't been in this room in months, she still left the door open. The clean scent of the paints greeted her as she crossed the threshold. She turned on the floor lamp beside the easel—a gift from her parents when she graduated from the art institute to replace her secondhand, falling apart one that had somehow got her through grad school. There was a work table with shelves pushed against the wall. The shelves were overflowing with containers of brushes and different types of paints, all colors of the rainbow. She painted in other mediums, but acrylic was her favorite.

She liked the thickness and texture of it, not to mention the vibrancy. Maybe that's why it had been so difficult to paint anything—her own life seemed to lack a certain amount of vibrancy these days.

She selected a brush, moving the soft hairs across the back of her hand. It wasn't that she hadn't tried to paint something new in all these months, it's just she would start and it would feel all wrong. The juxtaposition would be wrong, or the lighting off, the subject ill fit for the landscape. It was as if after things ended with Kevin, her mind became a mish-mashed mess. She smiled. That was an apt description. She turned the handle on the window's blinds, allowing some of the morning light to filter through. Moving fluidly about the room—she could navigate this room in her sleep—she picked up her palette and began to add various colors. Her easel already held a canvas that beckoned her every time she walked by the room, blank white eyes staring back at her.

Leaning against the stool beside her easel, she thought for a moment. Usually, she painted landscapes. Always realistic. The beach, the mountains, or the Buckeye trees in the fall. But this morning a very different image floated in her mind. She dabbed her brush into a purple-gray color of paint. Her dream—or her recollection depending on how you looked at it—had given her an idea. She began to brush in short, purposeful strokes. There was a veil between worlds, of that she was almost sure. Between the past and the present, of one life and the next. And for the briefest of moments she had experienced it.

She worked feverishly, consumed with the desire to not stop until the painting was finished. Her hands moved quickly and resolutely, knowing exactly which colors to create and where to place them on the canvas. By the time she was done, the morning sun had risen and bright golden light filtered through the window. Satisfied, she took a step back. The cool colors coalesced with the warm tones giving the canvas an earthy, yet ethereal affect. The blending of the colors so that they appeared seamless was the important part, like one life blending into the next. Was Adala's life blended into her life? Were there others?

She tilted her head examining her work. Out of the soft tones of the piece's background, the image of a woman's face appeared as if she was pushing herself out of the swirling colors, being birthed out of some kind of vortex. The woman's blonde curls were shoulder length, and Jenny had given her high cheekbones and a strong jawline, almost bordering on masculine. The lips were thin and unsmiling, but the critical piece was the woman's eyes. The face was almost a blur of soft, muted colors, but Jenny had taken the time to paint the eyes a deep, golden brown, careful to capture the right ratio of dark to light, giving them a fathomless quality. Those eyes clearly had a message to whoever viewed the painting. They said: *I have loved and I have lost. I am strong. I live on.* They were what had startled Jenny awake, haunting her in the brief moments between sleep and waking. Eyes that had seen both great horrors and insurmountable kindness.

Jenny smiled to herself before turning toward the hallway to let Caddie out and make some breakfast. She also wanted to call Meara and schedule another appointment. There were questions she had that only Meara would be able to help her answer. She glanced back at the first thing she had painted in months and the eyes of Adala seemed to smile back, as if whispering their approval.

# Chapter Twelve

"Oh my gosh, that's totally tragic," Hadley said as she speared a sautéed mushroom with her fork.

"I thought it was beautiful," Jenny responded picking at the remains of her gourmet chicken and feta pizza.

Hadley took a sip of her wine. "I agree. But, I mean, wow. Nothing I experienced was as involved as that. I mean, pretending to be Jewish to save someone's life? Her lover trying to save her and then being killed by the Nazis? It sounds like something out of a Nicolas Sparks movie."

Jenny had to agree. It did sound like something out of a movie, but at the same time it was her life. Well, one of them anyways. She played with the straw in her water glass, twirling it between her thumb and index finger. She'd called to make another appointment with Meara later that week. Of course, Meara didn't sound surprised in the least. For some reason, the one part Jenny hadn't shared with Hadley was what her Higher Self had to say and the lessons Jenny's soul was meant to learn. Instead she asked, "So, what were your lives like?"

"Well, you remember I only saw Meara for a few months. Every now and then she does e-mail me to ask how I'm doing, but as you already know, she's just like that." Hadley took another sip of wine. Her wavy blonde hair was especially rambunctious today and she was still wearing her leggings and cropped sweatshirt from yoga class earlier. "Basically, the lives that my Higher Self presented to me were ones that revealed my deep-rooted fears and anxieties about money and success. In one life, I was a successful businessman until the Great Depression, where I lost my job, then my family, and had to live in a Hooverville."

"One of those shanty towns of the thirties?" Jenny asked. "That would explain your fears about opening up your yoga studio."

Hadley nodded. "Exactly. And in another life I was an actress, not anyone famous or anything."

"Did you Google her?" Jenny interrupted.

"You bet your buns I looked her up. Mostly commercials, a few B movies. Pretty lady, but too much hairspray for my taste. Anyways, she ended up doing a lot of product endorsements in the days when 'We'll sue for you!' suddenly became everyone's favorite motto. Someone sued one of the companies over one of the products and she—I—ended up losing a really big deal. Eventually, I had to file bankruptcy."

"Did anything good come of it?"

"Actually, yes. I sold all of my belongings and moved to Hawaii with whatever I had left. I lived on the beach with my dog, surfing every day and selling coconut water and shell necklaces to tourists."

Jenny smiled. "That sounds a lot like you. Well, not the actress part, but the living on the beach part."

Hadley smiled too. "I know, right? There were a couple of others. But those were the two that stood out at the time because they seemed to reflect back to me the experience I was having at the time." She looked thoughtful for a moment. "I'm sure if I went back, I'd receive completely different messages."

"Did you learn anything about your Oversoul during the sessions?" The waiter brought their checks and

Jenny slipped her debit card into the holder.

Hadley scrounged around for cash in her oversized, slouchy purse. "Actually, I did. What I knew going in was stuff I'd already read about. How a soul will splinter off in order to learn its lessons more efficiently and that those soul pieces will gravitate toward one another, thus the whole idea of soulmates."

"Are we soulmates?" Jenny asked, even though she was pretty sure she already knew the answer. During the audio of her session, when she'd listened to her Higher Self describing how Keren went on to live a fulfilling life, Jenny could picture her deep brown eyes and jet black hair vividly. The slight tilt of her head and the defiance in her jaw—both the youth and the pride. And she realized who Keren reminded her of—the college version of Hadley.

Now, Hadley leveled her green eyes at Jenny. Jenny had always envied those eyes, they seemed almost fathomless at times. "Yes. I think we are. I know who you were to me in the lives of both the businessman and the actress." The waiter brought back their change and bid them a good evening. Jenny slipped her card back into her wallet and Hadley left the returned change as tip. "I think Jedd was too." She blushed a little at this. Jedd was

Hadley's boyfriend of almost a year. He was a great guy and a nice complement to Hadley's personality. If the saying opposites attract were true, then Hadley and Jedd were the proof.

Before she'd gone on this adventure, Jenny hadn't really thought about soulmates and what they were. She'd kind of just gone with the cookie-cutter belief that a soulmate was some wishful thinking, perfect, once-in-a-lifetime deal. But now she was questioning that notion. She knew Hadley was also Keren. And, based on the concept of an Oversoul, she now realized soulmates could take on many forms because souls played different roles in different lifetimes. In this incarnation Hadley was a lifelong best friend, one who'd felt like she'd known forever, and now, she knew, perhaps she had. In Adala's lifetime, the two had only known each other briefly, yet their lives were still inexplicably intertwined. She couldn't help but wonder if Kevin—or anyone else in her current life for that matter—were also part of the same Oversoul. If Krischen or Evert, or even the Commander were in this current lifetime alongside her? If they were, would she be able to recognize it? There was only one way to find out.

∞

Jenny's cell phone rang as she exited the parking garage. She noticed the still waiting envelope icon, indicating that she hadn't yet read the message from Kevin. The caller ID said that it was her mother. Jenny hit the green answer button and held the phone to her ear. She exited the parking garage and emerged onto the sunlit street. Meara's office was two blocks away. It was the middle of the afternoon and the sun was warm on her shoulders.

"Hi, Mom."

"Where are you?" That was typical of her mother. No greetings or pleasantries. Straight to business as usual.

"I'm downtown walking to an appointment. Why, what's up?" The lunch time rush was already over and the streets weren't overly busy. The usual business person here and there, or college kids with backpacks waiting to catch one of the RTA buses. She paused waiting for the traffic light to change green. The city had recently installed universal design crosswalks, ones that let out beeps for the visually impaired.

"Are you sick?" Her mother asked, something clanging in the background. She was recently retired and it seemed her mother could do with a hobby. It seemed

Jenny's life was becoming her hobby. Her father still worked most days since he owned his small graphic design firm and only had several employees. Besides, he enjoyed the work. And getting out of the house. For obvious reasons.

"No. I'm fine. Listen I'm almost there and the building has terrible reception," Jenny lied. "What's on your mind? Is everything okay?"

"Oh, everything's fine. I saw Sandra Allen at Zumba today. You went to school with her son, Graham."

Jenny shook her head as if her mother could see. "Not ringing any bells." She hurried across the street and picked up the pace toward the second block. Somehow hoping that the faster she walked, the sooner she'd get there and could end the phone call. She knew where this conversation was headed. It was headed in the same direction as always.

"Well, Graham has moved back home. He wants to live at home and save some money so he can buy a house of his own someday. Isn't that nice?" Another clang.

"Yeah, good for him."

"And," her mother's voice seemed to go up an octave. "Sandra said he's newly single."

"How convenient."

"You two could go out and grab a bite to eat. Catch up."

"I don't even remember who he is, Mom." The office building came into view, a looming beacon of freedom.

"Well, maybe once you saw him you would remember him. Look him up on that FacePlanner thing."

"You mean Facebook. Listen, I don't want to be someone's rebound relationship."

"You have to start somewhere, Jennifer. It's better than being nowhere." This time the clang was so deafening it caused a high pitch ringing in Jenny's ear.

"I'm at my appointment. Gotta go. Love you, bye." Jenny called into the phone as she pulled it away from her ear and hit the end button. She dropped her phone into her bag and ran up the front steps to the building.

Just like the other day, the lobby was nearly empty. Jenny pressed the button for the elevator. Graham Allen? The name truly didn't sound familiar. This was only the latest in a long list of potential Romeos that her mother had tried to line up. Jenny understood that she was only trying to help. Of course, she wanted her only daughter to be married and naturally she also wanted grandkids. And being an only child, there was no one else to displace some of the pressure. Her father took a more relaxed approach. He said everything would work out in its own time. But Jenny's mom seemed to have other ideas.

She stepped into the elevator and tapped the button for Meara's floor. What had her mother said before hanging up? *You have to start somewhere, Jennifer. It's better than being nowhere.* Was that true? Was she nowhere? She was making progress. She could feel it. Finally, seeing a painting through from beginning to end was a start. And seeking help from a professional—even if she was a regression therapist with a doctorate in metaphysics—was a start too. Maybe she had been nowhere for longer than she should have been, treading water in the vast sea of life. But she'd decided to take a chance and make a change, even if it was an unconventional one that her mother would never understand. She was looking at the bigger picture, at all the threads of the tapestry, not just a single thread. The elevator came to a grinding stop, its doors creaking open. Jenny stepped into the hallway and turned toward Meara's office once again. *You have to start somewhere.*

# Chapter Thirteen

Meara sat in the leather chair across from the chaise. She crossed her legs and examined her notes. She continued to act as if Jenny's return didn't surprise her in the least, and Jenny wondered if it was typical of Meara's clientele to first experience doubt only to put the pieces together and do an about face, or in Jenny's case at least a ninety degree turn.

"So, did you have any questions after reviewing the audio of your session?"

"More than I started with," Jenny quipped.

Meara's brow furrowed. Today she was wearing a sleek, elbow-length sleeved maxi dress and gold wedge heels. She looked like some sort of ancient goddess. "How so?" She wrote down notes as Jenny responded.

"Well, I'm beginning to understand the concept of the Oversoul. For example, I believe that Keren's soul is currently incarnated as Hadley. I don't know why I think that. I just do. It's like I just know."

Meara nodded. "Don't second guess the knowing. Your first instincts are usually the correct ones."

"I guess, I just wonder who are the other pieces?"

She nodded again. "Typically, those things are revealed in time. A certain knowing upon your next interaction, or sometimes a glimmer of recognition during the regression. And you'll see that the relations can be overlapped or mixed. For example, Hadley was someone you barely knew when you were Adala, yet now she is one of your longest and dearest friends. Your ex-boyfriend could be your father in a different existence—or even your mother."

"That's confusing."

Meara smiled. "Not if you think of the soul as genderless. It just is existence, in its purest sense. So it can take on any form. I once had a client describe a brief life as a tree. And even that had its lesson."

"Is that typical?"

"Not particularly, but it emphasizes the fact that whatever form will best teach the lessons needed is the one taken. Most often, we incarnate as human beings because of the sensory access." She peered down at her notes again. "Did you have any questions about the lessons learned from Adala's life?"

"No. I mean, I see how Adala rushed into love with Krischen."

*"Fools rush in."*

"Wasn't that a movie?"

"Actually, it's from an 18th century poem by Alexander Pope. But that aside, what else did Adala's life teach you?"

Jenny thought about it, carefully selecting the memories that stood out, as if they were now merged with her own memories, not two separate memories, but one. "One other thing. My Higher Self mentioned it, but I examined it a little further. I think Adala's life primarily shows that even at humanity's worst, it is often when we see humanity at its best. Like with the Commander and then both Adala and Evert."

*"Happiness can be found even in the darkest of times, if one only remembers to turn on the light."*

"Another 18th century poem?"

Meara grinned. "Harry Potter." Jenny smiled as Meara glanced through her notes again. "I have here that you wanted to explore the fear of being unlovable. Is this still something you wish to examine?"

Jenny thought about it. Did she think she was unlovable? It wasn't quite that. Well, maybe a little bit. But clearly Adala was lovable—she was loved by two men. Why then—in this life—was it so difficult for Jenny to find love? Was it simply a sign of the times and should she really resort to dating men her mother found out about while at Zumba? No. It wasn't the fear that she was unlovable. It was something more. The first life her Higher Self showed her allowed her to see that everyone has good and bad in them—including herself—but that it doesn't define who they are. Adala had an affair, but clearly that's not what she was remembered for. She was remembered for her sacrifice and her bravery. Her ability to rise up and be a beacon of justice in a time of great darkness.

"A life seems so simple. One life out of all the lives that have been lived and ever will be lived. And yet, it is so important. I've heard of the butterfly effect and always thought it kind of remarkable, but also unbelievable. A butterfly flaps its wings and can lead to a chain reaction that causes a tsunami on the other side of the world. How can one event have such a momentous impact?"

"Yes, I'm familiar with that theory."

"But a single life—no matter how short or long—is the same. One life is a single thread through the tapestry, but without that one thread, the tapestry doesn't make any sense."

"Are you saying you wish to examine something else with this regression?"

Jenny considered it. She did. "I want help in seeing the bigger picture."

"Can you be any more specific?" Meara continued to jot down notes, but a small smile played at the corners of her lips.

"I thought my own fears were preventing me from moving on. But it's not my fears that are stopping me, it's my inability to see the bigger picture. Adala, she could see the bigger picture. She knew the consequences for her actions, but she did it anyways. One small event had a momentous impact. I think I want to know the butterfly effect of my current incarnation."

Meara chuckled, but it was light-hearted, not belittling. "Well, I can only help you see your past lives and their effects on you. But perhaps your Higher Self will be able to provide more insight into your current situation."

Her mother's words came to mind. "You have to start somewhere."

"Indeed. Shall we begin then? Lay back and get comfortable. The sound of my voice will guide you into a deep state of relaxation. Allow your breath to become slow and even..."

# Chapter Fourteen

The first thing Jenny did was look down at her feet. Sandals. She was wearing flat-soled leather sandals that wrapped around her ankles. Her feet were tanned, much darker than her Irish-Welsh skin ever got, even when she vacationed in California. Her dress was long and made from a soft, silky fabric that moved along with her when she walked. It was bright orange in color with intricate beading around the hem. The walkway she was standing on was made of white cobblestones.

Her hair was in long, auburn curls well past her shoulders. She looked up at the sky, shielding her eyes from the glaring sun. The sky was cloudless and cerulean. She could hear the crash of waves in the near distance. She looked at her hands. She was holding a small basket full of seashells. Her hands were smooth and had long nails. There were no callouses. They were not working hands. They were young hands. She was maybe in her late teens. It was hard to tell. This body felt heavier—more solid—than Adala's. Jenny felt strong and alert, more than she ever had in her own body.

It was as though each time the first thing she noticed was the skin she was wearing. Then slowly, her surroundings would begin to come into focus. She was standing in a town square. The buildings around the square were made of white stone with colored cloth awnings. She noticed a grocer with stands of fruits and vegetables, and a weaver with elaborate tapestries hanging down. The individual stores had arched, open doorways.

"Menodora!" A woman called from behind her. Jenny turned and her eyes grew wide as she took in the giant columns behind her. Her eyes followed the columns upward toward the elaborate fresco just below the building's roof. A temple. "Menodora!" The woman called again. She was older, tanned from the prevalent sun, her hair graying around the temples and she also wore a long, one-shouldered dress. Her hair was long too, but the top of it was swept out of her face in elaborate braids. The woman paused in front of Jenny. She was holding a woven basket full of colorful flowers.

"I've been looking all over the square for you. Where have you been?" Jenny turned to see who the woman was speaking to, but no one else was there. *She must be speaking to me,* Jenny realized. *I am Menodora.* The woman's eyes were a pale blue with wrinkles at the corners. Even though she was older, she was exquisitely beautiful and carried herself in a regal manner. The eyes were familiar, but just as soon as Jenny thought it, it was gone.

The woman sighed. "Menodora, we do not need to purchase seashells from the merchants when our shores are abundant with them. Your heart is too big for your coin purse."

Menodora felt her cheeks flush. "I'm sorry, Mother. I know. I couldn't help it though. The child was so sweet, such large brown eyes."

"If a child with sweet eyes sold you something every time, we'd have a house full of useless things and not a coin to show for it." The woman chastised, but then her eyes softened. "We need not be frivolous. Your father and I are paying for a wedding in short time."

A wedding! That's right. She was getting married! But she couldn't recall to who. Not knowing what to say, Menodora apologized once again. "I am sorry, Mother." She stroked one of the shells in the basket. The sound of children playing in the square drifted to her ears coalescing with the sounds of the waves and the low drone of the merchants' voices, a cacophony of life.

"It's no matter. They will make lovely table decorations. Come, we must go. Pleagia will be waiting with your dress. Nikomedes is lucky he has found a wife with a heart such as yours. What does your father say?"

Menodora smiled. "That I have a heart bigger than Atlantis itself."

Sophia smiled, looping an arm through her daughter's. "I'm going to miss you, my Moon Child." Menodora had been born on the night of the full moon. Sophia had been told she wouldn't bear children. Theodotus had been disappointed, but to his credit he remained faithful to his barren wife. Sophia spent many nights praying to the goddess Artemis in the temple, hoping that their luck would change despite what the doctor had told them. When finally, after seven years of praying, Sophia found that she was with child. Of course it meant that her and Theodotus were older parents and were graced with only the one, but they couldn't have asked for a more beautiful daughter and were grateful to raise her. Sophia had insisted on naming her Menodora—gift of the moon. Theodotus was so happy at their change of fate, that he had no objections. It seemed only yesterday that she was born. Now, she was going to be married and starting a family of her own.

As if reading her mother's mind, Menodora smiled. "Weddings are such sad occasions."

"Sad, my dear?"

"Yes, don't get me wrong. They are happy too. But to leave behind what one has always known to embark on something new is always a little bit bittersweet."

"Oh, don't tell your father. His heart would be broken if he knew his little girl was sad about her wedding!" They exited the square and the buildings slowly became further apart and began to take on the appearance of dwellings. Emerald colored grass lined the cobblestone walkway and in the distance Menodora could see where the cerulean colored sky kissed the sapphire sea. Her heart soared with love for her home. She would never leave Atlantis. Ever.

"I am sad to leave you and Father, but happy to become Nikomedes' wife and a mother to children of my own."

Sophia smiled. How had she grown up so fast? She wished she could somehow slow down time and enjoy these last few moments with her daughter. "Come, I think I see Pleagia waiting for us!"

∞

Pleagia fixed the draped fabric that ran over Menodora's shoulders and down her back to the floor. The dress was a pristine white and it had golden jewels encrusted along the neckline and at the dress's hem. Pleagia had cinched an elaborate gold beaded belt at Menodora's waist. Then—ever so carefully—she had placed a headband of olive leaves dipped in liquid gold and then hardened—onto Menodora's head.

Now Menodora stood admiring herself in the mirror that leaned against the wall of her small bedroom in her parents' home. The whole affect was quite stunning. The contrast of the pure white silk of the dress against her tanned skin and the strands of her auburn colored hair, not to mention the piercing blue of her eyes that matched the sea just outside her window.

Pleagia stood next to her smiling. She was a bit shorter and squatter than Menodora, with slightly masculine features, nonetheless strong and beautiful. She wore a tan-colored dress that was almost an exact match to her own skin. Her hair was curly tendrils almost to her waist and a deep shade of chestnut brown. Her eyes were as striking as Menodora's but instead of sapphire, they were emeralds set deep into her face and flanked by long, dark lashes.

"You and your mother are miracle workers, Pleagia!" Menodora grinned, inspecting herself from all angles. "Nikomedes won't know what to do with himself."

"It is easy when the canvas is already so perfect, my friend." Pleagia smiled.

"How do you think I should wear my hair?" Menodora pulled her hair into an up-do, stretching her arms high above her head.

Just then the door opened and her mother appeared. "Oh, my goodness." A hand covered her mouth and she stifled a sob. "Your father will not be able to contain his emotions on your wedding day."

"Two days' time and I will soon be Menodora Karas." She smiled, but it didn't quite meet her eyes. She had thought of the name change frequently since her engagement. Karas meant *black* and Nikomedes meant *victorious plan*. Granted, names were just labels. Surely, it was simply an unfortunate choice in names.

Sophia admired her daughter's reflection. "And to answer your question. You should wear your hair down. It is quite beautiful and when you are raising children, you will find that you wish to keep it up and out of the way as little hands will often find it." She twirled her fingers between two strands of Menodora's loose curls. Then turned to Pleagia. "Tell your mother she does beautiful work. I must head back downstairs. Dinner needs to be ready before your father comes home. You girls enjoy your time together. Just be sure to return in time for dinner, Menodora." Sophia smiled, patted Pleagia gently on the shoulder, and exited the room.

Pleagia helped Menodora out of her wedding dress, draping it carefully over a chair in the corner of the room. Then took the headpiece and wrapped it in a cloth before placing it on the chair's seat cushion. Menodora shimmied back into her other dress. "Do you wish you were married, Pleagia?" she asked, flopping onto her bed and kicking her bare feet up into the air. The girls had known each other a long time. Atlantean girls were allowed schooling up until the age of fourteen, which they were then expected to help their mothers tend to the house and family. That chore was easy for Menodora considering she had no siblings. Her mother allowed her the extra time to pursue her own studies. She couldn't say the same for Pleagia.

Pleagia had a large family—at sixteen, she was the eldest of six children. The youngest was still practically fresh out of the womb. When she had to stop schooling, she had to help her mother take care of the children and she had to learn her mother's trade of dressmaking, which luckily Pleagia enjoyed immensely.

Ignoring Menodora's question. She said instead, "The beading at the hem was my idea. And down the center of the dress's back. A woman should look just as good coming as she does going. Don't you think?"

"Ah!" scolded Menodora. "Don't avoid the question."

Pleagia sighed, slumping into the other chair opposite the bed. "Sometimes I think I would want that. To be married and have a husband. It would be nice to leave behind the chaos of my brothers and sisters. But what if my husband would not allow me to work? I love creating beautiful dresses and making women feel like the goddesses they are deep inside!"

Menodora nodded. "Indeed. You do make them feel like a goddess. I felt like Aphrodite herself!" Then she giggled.

Pleagia giggled too. "Zeus would be jealous." This caused both girls to fall into a fit of laughter. Menodora rolled over onto her stomach so that she was facing Pleagia directly, her face suddenly serious.

"Pleagia, do you think I am crazy? I think I love Nikomedes, but I cannot be sure. I hardly know him truthfully, but I trust my parents to pick me a proper husband. And yet, there is this nagging feeling deep in here—" She gestured toward her stomach. "That something is not quite as it seems."

Her friend looked at her thoughtfully, biting her bottom lip. "No, I do not think you're crazy. But I don't know how to advise you either. You're right. I don't know enough about Nikomedes to judge his character. He is a man of wealth and well-respected."

"Well-respected or well-feared?" Menodora asked.

"Either way, would you disobey your parents' wishes?"

Menodora sighed. "No, I don't think that I could do that."

"Then the answer is final."

"I am excited for the wedding. But that is my concern. Am I excited only for the wedding and not for the marriage itself? How can you think you love someone? You either love them or you do not love them."

"Love is not such a simple thing as to be so black and white." Pleagia's voice was soft. Menodora stared out the window. They were on the second floor and her bedroom faced back toward the town square. In the distance she could see the Temple of Artemis, glowing in the light of the setting sun. Artemis was the goddess of the moon and of the virgin. That much they had in common. Perhaps the goddess could provide some guidance.

Pleagia followed her gaze out the window to the temple glowing in the light of the rising moon.

"I think I have an idea," Menodora smiled.

# Chapter Fifteen

When the moon was high and full, nestled against the midnight sky, Menodora carefully draped her cloak about her shoulders. She pulled the hood loosely up and over her auburn hair. Barefoot was best for fear that her sandals would make a sound against the stone floor. She crept down the steps, careful to tread on her toes so that she wouldn't create the sound of skin slapping against the stone. The house was eerily silent as she made her way through the front room and down the hallway to the arched wooden doorway. As quietly as she could, she pulled the door open, stepped into the cool breeze of the night, and shut the door silently behind her.

The town was quiet, even the animals were asleep. The stillness seemed to amplify the sound of the crashing waves from the sea. No birds called out at this time of night. The moon was a large white globe casting its light like a lantern. The plan was to go around the outskirts of the town square, near where Pleagia's family resided, then together they would head to the Temple of Artemis.

Menodora shivered in the cool breeze, inciting a rash of goose flesh up and down her arms. Pleagia's family home was east of the markets. It was more farm-like than her own home, just on the outskirts of the town. She walked briskly for maybe a half mile before coming upon the stone wall that marked the far edge of the Rokos' property. The horses were in their stalls fast asleep and the sheep were in a small huddle lying in the grass. Pleagia sat on the wall waiting.

"You're early," Menodora said.

"You're late," Pleagia replied. The light of the moon created a halo around her dark head, softening her masculine features and making her appear almost ethereal. She hopped off the wall, pulling a satchel down along with her. The satchel contained the items they would place on the goddess' altar.

The girls were best friends and even though Menodora's father was in the Senate and her family a bit wealthier, and even though Pleagia had five other siblings and Menodora was an only daughter, they found they had a lot in common. Both girls were curious and smart, sometimes so much so that they had gotten into trouble. Like the time when they were seven and decided to take two of the Rokos' horses and ride to the sea in order to see the ships sailing through the Pillars of Hercules. Or the time when instead of going to school and learning their lessons, they'd snuck away to the cove on the other side of the outer ring and went swimming in the crystalline waterfalls. Yes, they were a pair of paradoxes. One stubborn and one unconditionally loving. One was a leader and the other a natural-born follower. Both were adventurers through and through. And whenever Menodora's head was too high up in the clouds, Pleagia was always there to pull her back down again. They were best friends, but long ago had decided they were sisters by choice.

The two girls, now nearly women, walked hurriedly down the cobblestone path that wound around the center of the only town either had ever known. The full moon lit their way. Menodora's hand slipped into Pleagia's. Her friend gave it a reassuring squeeze as she glanced back, her emerald eyes dancing with excitement.

Menodora stifled a giggle. Together they ran, barefoot and hand-in-hand, their hearts full of childlike wonder and innocence toward the Temple of Artemis, which glowed ominously in the distance.

∞

The Temple of Artemis wasn't for the faint of heart. The path leading up to the temple opened onto a courtyard with a stone water fountain. In its center was a horse reared up on its hind legs, a beautiful maiden holding a bow and arrow astride its back. Water shot up into the air out of the horse's mouth and splashed back down into the surrounding pool. There were shrubs of brilliantly colored flowers—hibiscus—and statues of playful looking children lined either side of the path leading up to the temple's steps. After all Artemis was both the goddess of fertility and of the hunt. It only seemed fitting

Giant lanterns flanked either side of the steps that led into the temple. The two young women padded quietly up the front steps, undaunted by the beautiful fresco spread above the entrance to the temple. The fresco showed Artemis atop a stallion, her bow and arrow poised at the ready, a flock of maidens and various woodland creatures stood behind her. The fresco always made Menodora stop and take note of the naturalness of being a woman. How the women and animals seemed to stand together in solidarity alongside their goddess, ready and willing to do her bidding.

Hundreds of limestone pillars, as wide round as four women, lined the temple. At the base of each pillar was an inset floor lamp that stayed continuously lit thanks to the dim glow of the special algae that grew in the nearby sea. The lights created an upward glow so that the pillars were brilliantly lit at their base and then their tops disappeared into the darkness of the temple's ceiling. The pillars held up the roof that protected the statue of Artemis and the altar inside, but they also seemed to stand sentry. When Menodora was little she used to imagine that at night the pillars would come to life in order to protect the goddess inside.

Pleagia led the way through the temple, past the stems of flowers that were scattered about, offerings tossed aside in haste, until they reached the center of the temple, where the statute of Artemis was located. The statue was massive, easily sixty feet in height. Unlike the rest of the temple, the lighting here was down lit, bathing Artemis in a ray of golden light. The goddess always took Menodora's breath away. She was made of solid gold, down to every finger and toe. She was barefoot and wearing a flimsy dress that hit above her knee. She had a quiver slung over her shoulder and held a bow facing down, in her right arm. Her head was turned upward slightly, so that there seemed a jaunty set to her jaw. She was voluptuously proportioned and her hair tumbled past her shoulders until it reached her breasts. A woodland bird sat on her left shoulder as if whispering in her ear and a fawn lay curled up at her feet. She was both frightening and magnificent.

"When I was a little girl," Pleagia whispered, sinking to her knees in front of the statue, "I used to imagine she was my mother."

Menodora lowered herself down beside her best friend, flipping the hood of the cloak back off her head so that her hair fell softly around her face. "What's wrong with the mother you have?"

Pleagia smiled. "Not a thing. But she was always busy with all of my brothers and sisters. I don't know. I've always felt a connection of some kind to Artemis. Out of all of our goddesses, she is the one I revere the most."

Menodora smiled, fingering at the ashen remains that littered the altar at Artemis's feet. "You and every man and woman on Atlantis."

"True." Pleagia slipped a small, white cloth out of her satchel and began to dust away the sacrificial remains of the altar so that they could have a clean workspace.

The moon spilled between the pillars in such a way that it cast a band of light across Artemis's bosom and landed on the floor a few feet away to her right. Menodora rummaged through the satchel and pulled out the bundle of sage that would be used to clear the energy of the space. She pulled out a fire starter and lit the end of the bundle, the pungent, bitter earthy smell immediately filling her nostrils. Once a good flame was established she blew it out so that the sage would only burn, releasing its purifying affects into the surrounding space. It was important to clear the space before they made offerings of their own. They didn't want their wishes mixed with the wishes of someone else, especially someone who had ill-intent. Pleagia handed her a peacock feather and an abalone shell from her satchel. Menodora placed the burning bundle carefully into the shell's small basin then walked carefully around the statue of Artemis, moving counterclockwise, waving the sage smoke with the feather and chanting softly: *Goddess of the moon I ask that you clear this space of negativity and instead replace it with the pureness of light and love.*

As Menodora smudged the space, Pleagia placed three white votive candles along the altar. Next she reached into the satchel, which was now nearly empty, and pulled out a cluster of moon flower blossoms. Moon flower was abundant on Atlantis. The flowers thrived in the tropical climate and their vines were known to meander around many houses in and around the village. The giant, white petals of the flower only bloomed by the light of the moon, as if soaking in the transformative beauty that only the lunar goddess could offer, before sealing itself up tight during the daylight hours. Pleagia arranged the blossoms carefully around the votive candles and just as she finished, Menodora came back around the opposite side of the statue. She placed the abalone shell carefully at the end of the altar, allowing the sage bundle to burn itself out. She laid the peacock feather down on the altar as an offering, after all she was not only the goddess of the hunt, but the goddess of the natural world, which to Menodora meant of all things pure and beautiful.

"Let's hurry, before the full moon begins to set," Pleagia said. She pulled one last thing out of the satchel. It was a worn, blue leather-bound book that was tied closed with a matching blue ribbon. Pleagia's fingers skillfully untied the ribbon, as if she'd tied and untied it many times before. Probably because she had. The book was a treasure from the childhood of the two fledgling women, who now sat shoulder to shoulder at the feet of Artemis. The tome contained stories that the women wrote as young girls, stories that they used to write to one another, and finish for one another. Stories of friendship, exploration, alien worlds and, of course, love. Interspersed among the stories were enchantments and prayers the girls would write in preparation for their late night visits to the temple of their favorite goddess.

Pleagia deftly flipped through the pages, searching for something in particular. When she found it she let out a happy sigh. "Here, this is the one."

Menodora looked over her shoulder. "Are you sure?"

"Of course, I'm sure. Have I ever led you wrong before?"

## Chapter Sixteen

The two days' time passed quickly. Menodora awoke to the sun shining brightly in through the window, bathing the room in its golden brilliance. Her beautiful beaded, silk wedding dress was still draped over the back of the chair from where Pleagia had left it after the fitting. Today was the day. By sun down she would be a married woman. Menodora Karas, wife of Nikomedes. Her stomach roiled, but she chocked it up to nervousness. Even though she played like she didn't mind it, Menodora didn't really like being the center of attention and that's exactly what she would be today. All eyes would be on her as the only daughter of Theodotus and Sophia, *and* she was to be wed to the seventh son of a seventh son. What were the odds?

Even though Menodora was an only child, her extended family was fairly large. Probably at least a quarter of the island, if not more were somehow related to her mother or her father. And with Nikomedes being the seventh child of a seventh child, at least another quarter of the island would represent the Karas family. Not to mention her father's role in the Senate. She closed her eyes against the morning sun and sighed. At least half the island would appear to be in attendance at today's wedding.

The early hours were at least reserved for her alone. It was supposed to be the bride's time for self-reflection as she moved from maiden to matron. Then, per tradition, her mother would bring her breakfast accompanied by her fellow maids, which consisted of cousins and other relatives with whom she didn't really associate, but who were all too willing to participate in the tradition of tricking the evil spirits and warding off any bad luck. Her mind drifted back to the night at the Temple of Artemis and the enchantment Pleagia had decided upon. The enchantment was one meant to calm her nerves, but instead it seemed to have the opposite effect. For the last two days, Menodora could swear she'd had a heightened sense of awareness, that things around her appeared to somehow be moving slower through time and space.

Just yesterday she had been walking through the market when she saw a child playing with a simple stick and hoop sort of game. As the child ran past, it was as if everything had slowed down and the boy stared right at her with his joyful, deep set brown eyes. A moment frozen in time. And then as quick as it had occurred, everything seemed to return to normal again as if nothing strange had even happened.

And then the day before that, she'd been having her final preparation meeting with the high priestess who would oversee the marriage ceremony. Her parents were alongside her as they ate a simple dinner of fish, vegetables, and goat cheese with some wine from the priestess's own vineyard, discussing the last minute details. The high priestess lived along the sea on a sprawling section of land, a gift from the Senate that showed their reverence for the priestess and the protection she brought to their island home. Some traditions seemed older than time itself. As they talked, Menodora's mind had begun to drift and she had stared out at the sun setting beyond the sea. The sky was all shades of indigo, tangerine, and magenta. However, for the briefest of instances, she could have sworn the magenta turned a garish red, the tangerine a fiery orange, and the indigo a deadly black. She'd gasped and dropped her fork. But then she had blinked and it was if she'd imagined it. After multiple reassurances, her parents attributed it to an unassuming case of wedding nerves.

Menodora wasn't so sure. She hadn't told anyone, especially Pleagia. She didn't want Pleagia to worry about her or think she had caused her friend undue stress before her big day. Except. Menodora opened her eyes and rolled herself out of bed. She grabbed a nearby shawl and draped it over her shoulders, stepping out onto the small balcony just outside her bedroom window. The sun was still low in the sky. It was early, much earlier than she would normally wake. The sky was bathed in pink and gold. She could hear birds twittering in the distance, as well as the soft crash of the sea. She took a deep breath, inhaling the fresh salt air which always seemed to calm her nerves. It was going to be a long day. After her mother and her bridesmaids appeared there would be hours of getting ready, the ritual foot washing, and the salt bath to rid her of impurities for her wedding night. Then her mother would present her to her father where the high priestess would then bless all three of them with the sacred oil. After that there would be a procession through the town's square and to one of the three bridges that led from the outer island ring and into the second ring's town square. Once they passed through that town's square, they would then take the last bridge to the center ring where the wedding ceremony would be performed.

Atlantis was made up of three concentric island rings. The outer ring was where the farms and fishing villages were primarily located—one of the reasons the Temple of Artemis was also located there. The outermost ring is where Menodora lived. Many merchants, several temples, and numerous government buildings were housed on the middle island ring. And the innermost ring contained the capital city and held the Temples of Zeus, Poseidon, and Aphrodite. The courtyard of the Temple of Aphrodite would be where Menodora and Nikomedes would be wed. In the center of the innermost ring was Mount Ignis—the Mountain of Fire. The three temples surrounded this mysterious mountain that the Atlanteans knew little about. They knew at one time it had spewed fire from its top, but the Atlantean scientists were confident that had been millennia ago. Menodora recalled learning in school that Mount Ignis had even formed the concentric rings of Atlantis, but she couldn't remember how.

As she stared off into the sky, she caught notice of something peculiar. A brilliant ball of light seemed to soar across the sky, as if somehow falling from the heavens and traveling down to the earth below, a fiery tail blazed behind it. She watched as it seemed to disappear below the horizon. Was it another one of the weird things she had been noticing the last couple of days? Perhaps a sign of some kind? Or maybe she had only imagined it. But even she didn't believe that was the case. She knew what she had seen. It could be a blessing, she decided.

Or worse. A warning.

∞

The house was so full of guests that they spilled out into the yard. Menodora found the entire ordeal overwhelming. Luckily, she had Pleagia there. She wasn't family, but she was the closest thing Menodora had to a sister and therefore it was easy to persuade her parents to let Pleagia be a bridesmaid and spend the day by her side. She had smiled politely as people—some she was pretty sure she'd never even met before—told her how lovely she looked, and continued to smile as she'd been hugged and kissed by more people than she could count.

Only two parts of the morning had moved her to

tears. One, being when she was finally dressed in her beautiful silk, beaded dress with the gold-dipped olive leaf crown placed upon her auburn curls. Pleagia had stood beside her admiring her handiwork in the mirror, wearing her own gown of deep green that matched her emerald eyes. With her brown hair and gemstone eyes, Pleagia looked as if she truly could be Menodora's sister, not simply a sister of the heart. For some reason the reflection of their heart-shaped faces staring back at her caused the backs of her own eyes to burn with tears.

And the second time was when her father saw her for the first time. Theodotus seemed to positively beam with the light of Apollo's sun. Menodora was close to her mother, but make no mistake she was definitely her father's daughter, his pride and his joy. They'd hugged and she hadn't even cared that the tears caused her ashen berry eyelash makeup to run trails down her cheeks. Sophia had clucked her disapproval, then set about fixing her daughter's makeup.

Before the procession to the center ring would begin, her father would ceremoniously paint kaolin clay across her face: two thumbprints in the shape of a heart in the center of her forehead and a small white triangle on either cheek symbolizing the past, present, and future of the bride-to-be. But Menodora preferred to think of the triangle as representing their tight knit family of three.

Once her father was done and they said a prayer to Aphrodite for her love and grace on such a special occasion, the musicians picked up their processional march. The low beat of the drum coalesced with the soft strum of the guitar and the high-pitched trill of the bone flute. The bridesmaids and other wedding guests began to clap in time to the music, whooping with delight. By this time, the sun had lowered in the sky creating a wash of golden light across the dancers. Pleagia handed her a bouquet of violet and fuchsia bougainvillea flowers. Her father looped his arm through hers and they made their way out the front door and into the night of the evening.

The path leading to the bridge, wound through the town square. People stopped what they were doing and smiled at the large processional, some even stopped to clap their hands along to the music. A few of the bridesmaids diverged from the procession in order to loop arms with the villagers and turn them about in a little dance. There were several distant cousins, young children, who were part of the processional and would run ahead of the group, tunic tails and curly tendrils already loosened and the ceremony itself had yet to begin.

Pleagia never strayed too far from her side. Occasionally, she cast a glance of concern Menodora's way, noting her friend's hesitance and perhaps realizing it wasn't simply a case of pre-wedding nervousness. Townspeople stopped to kiss Sophia's cheeks and some—hearing the celebration before it reached them—tossed golden coins into the air as signs of prosperity, a time-old Atlantean tradition.

They reached the bridge in what seemed like no time at all. The bridge linking the outermost ring of fisheries and farms to the middle ring of council and merchants was made of limestone. It had beautiful arches beneath it that reflected in the cerulean sea. Its four tall posts—two on either side—were topped with carvings and tropical flowers spilled down their sides. Even the bridges were exquisite and intricate in their beautiful detail. Just like everything in Atlantis.

The children led the way over the bridge and the processional followed. Each island was smaller than the previous so it didn't take very long to follow the winding path through the center of town. The sun continued its slow descent. They would reach the Temple of Aphrodite just as the sun hovered over the horizon, then after the ceremony there would be dancing and merriment long into the hours of the night.

In contrast to the outermost ring, the buildings of the second most ring were pushed together in tight clusters. To Menodora it felt claustrophobic. The town's square didn't have the same familial quality as home, but it was nonetheless beautiful. Colorful tropical flowers and elaborate fountains adorned the small temple of Plutus, the God of Prosperity, at the center of the island. They passed through, nodding their head to the villagers watching the procession. Her father wore a smile that was ear-to-ear and her mother was clearly enjoying the attention that came with being the mother-of-the-bride, and she looked every bit the part in her long, plum-colored gown that trailed behind her, layers of silver and gold beading adorning her neck, and stacks of metallic bangles lining her wrists. Menodora had chosen to keep things more simple: only wearing small pearl earrings and a gold cuff on her arm—a wedding gift from her father.

Before she knew it they had reached the second—and final—bridge that led into the third and innermost ring. The bridge was in the same style as the last with limestone statues, and fountains of flowering vines. The sun was almost to the horizon and the darkening sky turned the cerulean sea into a shade of indigo. The evening sky was ablaze in rubies, amethysts, and topazes. A bejeweled sky for a bejeweled bride. The children's laughter floated back to her and the sounds of the guitar, drum, and flute seemed to quicken in pace. On the other side of that bridge, Nikomedes, his family, and his friends would be awaiting her arrival. Menodora took a deep breath and felt a gentle nudge from behind. She turned. Pleagia smiled, her eyes encouraging. Because Pleagia knew. She knew that the enchantment from the full moon would work and that if this marriage wasn't meant to be it wouldn't be, and if it were meant to be, then the goddess Artemis would bestow them with blessings beyond measure. At least there was no doubt in her friend's mind.

Menodora thought of the blackened sky from the day before and the fiery ball of light she saw earlier that very morning. Were they signs that it shouldn't be? Or signs of the blessings to come? Her heart seemed to know what her mind refused to acknowledge. She let her father guide her across the bridge and into the innermost ring of Atlantis.

This was it.

# Chapter Seventeen

The courtyard was bathed in a pool of golden light. Intricate topiaries carved into winding shapes flanked the marble stairway leading down to the center of all three temples. Naturally, Zeus's temple was grandest, topped with a fresco done in gold filigree. To its left sat the Temple of Poseidon, up-lit in a wash of soft blue light. To the right sat the temple of Aphrodite, glowing softly in a delicate pink. Each temple had rows upon rows of columns and Menodora knew if she were to enter into any of them, she would be greeted by a massive statue of the respective god or goddess whose house of worship was entered.

In the center of the courtyard was a giant fountain, a tribute to Atlantis. In its center was Zeus and in his open palm was a sphere. The sphere had three rings around it so to the untrained eye it would almost appear to be a planet of some sort. But it wasn't. It was the representation of Atlantis. A gift from the highest of gods himself and bestowed upon the Earth so that man could thrive. Atlantis was gifted with wealth from Pluto, bounty from Demeter, water for energy thanks to Poseidon, and a growing population thanks to Aphrodite and Artemis. Atlantis was surely a gift from the gods because there simply was no other explanation for its existence.

Behind the three temples and the courtyard loomed Mount Ignis—the Mountain of Fire. It was purple-gray in color, almost appearing dull compared to the lush, vibrantly colored surrounding landscape. Menodora and her father paused at the top of the steps, taking in the majesty of the innermost ring. Indeed, to be an Atlantean was akin to being royalty. Finally, Menodora's eyes rested on Nikomedes who stood waiting in a knee length toga of white fabric, the same style of golden beading as her own dress flanking his shoulder. Pleagia's mother had made his ceremony attire. He too wore a crown of gold-dipped olive leaves which glinted in the light of the quickly setting sun. His blonde hair was windswept, even though there was no wind and his jaw was set defiantly.

The family of Nikomedes stood waiting and Theodotus gave his daughter a gentle nudge. The music that had only moments before been so rapid, began to slow, the beginning of the marital march. Menodora's bridesmaids carefully made their way down the steps, following the children. Pleagia turned to look at her friend, tilting her head slightly, eyes suddenly worried. Perhaps she had been wrong. As Pleagia and then Sophia made her way down the steps, Nikomedes met Sophia part way to escort her to her spot near where Menodora would stand, the sky was aflame in pulsating colors of red, orange, and deep indigo. The wedding march segued into the bride's song and Menodora took a breath and let it out slowly as her father began to guide her down the stairs and into the courtyard.

Just as her sandal hit the marble of the courtyard, the earth beneath her feet let out a low rumble of protest. She almost lost her balance, gripping her father's arm, but he too was doubled over. She looked up at Nikomedes whose calm collectedness had all but vanished, replaced with an expression that was a mix of both anger and fright.

"Father, what's happening?" Menodora managed

to ask as the temples seemed to moan with the shake of the earth. A topiary in a ceramic pot right beside Menodora toppled over, crashing into pieces on the marble surface, dirt spilling out. And then another crash. The women cried out, rushing toward their children. Men shouted out, but Menodora couldn't make sense of what they were saying.

Theodotus stumbled backward, falling onto the hard surface and bringing Menodora, who was still gripping his arm, tumbling over him, causing a loud rip through the length of her skirt as her sandal caught and she fell to her knees. Pleagia came running over and grabbed her arm.

"Pleagia, please. What is happening?" Menodora whispered, more than a little frightened.

"Look!" Pleagia's voice was barely audible over the rumble coming from deep within the earth. Menodora looked up in the direction that Pleagia pointed. Mount Ignis. It was as if the mountain was splitting open from the inside out, only Menodora couldn't figure out if it was the mountain splitting the earth or the earth splitting the mountain.

"Father! What do we do?" Menodora cried out, but there was no answer. Theodotus had smacked his head when he had fallen and Sophia now kneeled with his head cradled in her lap, a trickle of blood dripping onto her dress. Menodora and Pleagia rushed to her side.

"Nikomedes! Help us!" Menodora called to her almost husband, but when she turned around she didn't see him. "Nikomedes?"

"Over there," Pleagia cried nodding her head in the direction of the bridge. Women carrying children clasped in their arms and several men—among them Nikomedes—ran across the bridge, heading back to the outermost rings.

"Perhaps he's going to warn the others." Menodora hoped, yet the words seemed false even as they left her lips.

"Perhaps, he's running away like the coward that he is." Menodora turned locking eyes with Pleagia.

"This," she said. One word. But one word could speak volumes betwixt best friends who were almost sisters.

Pleagia nodded. "This."

∞

Mount Ignis was angry. The ground rumbled beneath their feet. Could this truly be because the union between Menodora and Nikomedes was not meant to be?

Yet, if she had wanted a sign there was none clearer than this. The evening sky had darkened quickly from indigo to black. Gray ash shot up and out of the volcano, raining down on them, coating their hair and sticking to their eyelashes.

Together Pleagia, Sophia, and Menodora helped Theodotus to his feet. He was still unstable, but conscious, as the shaking continued. There was a loud *crack* followed by a *crash*! Menodora turned to see the pillars inside the Temple of Zeus beginning to give way. The temple stood sentry at the mountain's base. The crashing of the pillars was like the effect of so many children's blocks being smashed to the ground. The gods were angry. Why, Menodora didn't know, but this was their consequence.

Without communicating, Pleagia and Menodora each scooped one of Theodotus's arms into their own, leveraging him so that his feet barely touched the ground. Sophia led the way—she was fast and strong despite her age. She ran in the direction of the limestone bridge that led to the next outer ring, the two best friends were close on her heels. Theodotus's head sagged, his chin near his chest, as he seemed to go in and out of consciousness. But there was no time. They had to get as far away from the spewing beast as possible. And that meant the outermost ring. Home. If they were lucky, those who had fled before them would tell the others and ships would be ready by the time they reached the sea. Ready and waiting to take them as far away as possible from the wrath of the gods.

Menodora's sandals pounded so hard against the marble and limestone that the soles of her feet stung. The bridge was barely intact when they reached it. Several of the ornaments and potted plants had tumbled, and a large chunk out of the center arch was gone…fallen into the sea.

"Hurry!" Sophia called. And the girls ran after her, dragging the old man the best they could, over the quickly deteriorating bridge. As soon as their feet landed on the other side—onto the land of the middle ring—another large chunk of the bridge cracked off in protest, falling into the hungry sea. The women's breath came in quick bursts. People stepped out of their homes, confused, staring at the great mountain in a combination of shock and wonder.

The ash continued to rain down, coating everything—rooftops, people, the cobblestone street. It looked like a scene from a book she'd read—as if they'd been transported to another world. The people who didn't stare in bewilderment, began to run too, abandoning whatever they had been doing, and soon the three women and Theodotus were joined by a small group of people. The cobblestone was slippery from the ash and Menodora slipped, falling to one knee and further tearing her dress. Her father and Pleagia would have fallen down with her if a young man hadn't stopped and scooped Theodotus up, tossing him over his shoulder as if he were a simple rag doll.

"Thank you!" Menodora said.

The man said nothing, just nodded, and the only thing Menodora would recall about him were his cornflower-colored eyes in his ash covered face. Pleagia grabbed her hand and the two women ran after Sophia, slipping and sliding along the ash, which was rapidly thickening. No more vibrant rainbow of plants and no more lush gardens, everything now a sea of gray. They were nearing the last bridge, the bridge that would lead them home and to the sea where Menodora was sure ships would already be waiting.

Except when they reached the bridge it was already gone. Nothing but two posts on either side. If she squinted she could see her mother on the other side. Some people were already swimming the short distance across. Atlanteans were strong swimmers, they were people of the sea. But the sea was churning wildly as if it no longer wanted to be contained in the precise channels that had been created for it.

"Come!" Pleagia urged pulling her toward the shoreline, her dress was covered in such a thick layer of ash that you couldn't even tell it had once been emerald. Her hair was also gray and her face smeared with a combination of dirt, ash, and dried blood.

Menodora waded into the cold water of the sea. The current was strong. Was there no god left un-angered? Water rushed at her legs and when her toes could no longer reach the bottom she began to swim in long, careful strokes. It was only about a quarter mile to the other side, but the water pushed and pulled from every direction. She watched as another woman swimming beside her seemed to lose her energy, she began to be pulled away by the current, Menodora reached out—knowing that she could be pulled away by the current too—and her fingertips brushed against the woman's, water streaked her face creating lines of color through the ash, but the woman couldn't hold on and she was swept away by the current, carried out to the vast sea.

Menodora felt sick to her stomach. She knew this was not their fault. That she and Pleagia had not summoned this kind of disaster on their fellow Atlanteans, but she also couldn't pinpoint what had angered the gods so much that their world was being destroyed before their very eyes. She closed her eyes and swam with fierce, purposeful strokes toward the shoreline. When her feet could touch the bottom, she walked and Pleagia already waited on the shore, her hand outstretched. Menodora grasped the familiar fingers and the strong hand pulled her onto dry land.

"I couldn't save her," Menodora managed between gasps.

"It is your duty to save yourself, my friend," Pleagia rationalized. "Come. Let's hope there are ships waiting."

Pleagia pulled Menodora along, the bottom of her dress had completely ripped off and all that remained was a ragged line above her knee. Menodora stumbled to keep up with Pleagia's long strides.

"My father," Menodora gasped. "How will we find him?"

"He will be fine," Pleagia reassured her.

"You don't know that."

"I don't need to know. My hope is enough."

"Hope cannot save us from the anger of the gods."

Pleagia turned toward her friend. "If not hope, then what? When all is lost, hope is all that remains."

Menodora didn't respond this time. She just squeezed her best friend's hand as the world around them seemed to crumble, the sky crashing angrily down and the ground opening hungrily beneath them. If this was the end of the world, there wasn't anyone else she'd rather have by her side. Friends by chance. Sisters by choice.

# Chapter Eighteen

Meara clicked her pen several times. Jenny's breathing had slowed and she knew that she was going to be transitioning out of the lifetime of Menodora. She gave it a few minutes before she began asking questions to Jenny's Higher Self. If she was being frank, she was a little unnerved by Jenny's past life experiences, at least the ones that were being revealed to her. It would seem Jenny lived during several catastrophic moments in history. Her soul was proving to be quite an evolved one.

Finally, she asked, "So, Atlantis is real then?"

"Yes, just past the Pillars of Hercules existed a three-ring island betwixt Eurasia and Africa," the Higher Self responded.

"And Mount Ignis, it was the volcano that destroyed their civilization?"

"Indeed. A meager number of Atlanteans were able to sail away, heading toward Eurasia. However, even fewer actually survived the journey."

"I was wondering about Pleagia. Is Pleagia someone that Jenny is currently incarnated with?"

The tone of the reply seemed as if it were smiling when it answered. "Yes. Hadley is the current incarnation of Pleagia. Hadley and Jenny have had many incarnations together. Our souls enjoy each other's company."

"That doesn't surprise me," Meara smiled. As much as she enjoyed listening to the details of her patients' other existences, her discussion with the Higher Self always gave her the most pleasure. The Higher Self was something—someone—that was so readily available, and yet so few people accessed it. In the times of the Atlanteans and even the Ancient Greeks and Romans, it wasn't uncommon to interact with other planes of existence. Even the Buddha meditated for seven years in order to access this sacred bond. Now, it seemed people were ridiculed for being spiritual; however, Meara could sense that a shift was occurring. People were becoming sick of the status quo and seeking a return to living with deeper meaning. This made her own soul very happy. The work she was doing was important. It mattered. "And what about Sophia? Is Sophia someone Jenny incarnates regularly with?"

"In this instance, the relation was the same."

"So Sophia is currently incarnated as Jenny's mother?"

"Yes."

"Is there something Jenny learned about her mother from experiencing this life?"

"Both Jenny's mother and Menodora's mother are preoccupied with marriage, not so much for the sacredness of it, but for the simple act. Nikomedes was not worthy a suitor for Menodora. He proved to be selfish and uncaring. If the tragedy hadn't struck, Sophia would have seen this, but as the fates would have it the gods had other plans that day."

"Has Mrs. McClain's soul learned from this pattern?"

"The pattern has not yet ceased. Therefore, the lesson is still being worked on."

"Is there anything your soul can do to help her mother's soul learn from this pattern?" Meara feverishly jotted down notes in her book, the pen scratching softly across the fresh pages.

"Be ourself."

Meara paused, confused. "Can you elaborate?"

"When our soul learns its lessons in this incarnation, so too will her mother's soul."

"I see," Meara looked thoughtfully out the window at the overcast sky, the Cleveland skyline loomed in the near distance. "Are there other lessons Jenny can learn from her incarnation as Menodora?"

There was a long pause, as if the Higher Self was considering the proper response. At last it said, "The fall of Atlantis was an important moment in history. There is so little known about the civilization since it was all but obliterated. Only stories and dreams of it seem to exist. However, the people of Atlantis were very real. Pleagia and Menodora had the bond of sisters, even though no common blood ran through their veins. Pleagia had many biological brothers and sisters, but the bond between her and Menodora was stronger. Menodora felt chosen by Pleagia, which the love of a chosen sister spoke to her greater than if she had been her genetic sister. This love—and the subsequent sisterly bond—forever tied their two souls together. When Menodora was incarnated as Adala, her soul remembered this bond. It is why she so readily sacrificed her life for the life of Keren, whom at the time she barely knew. We may not always recognize one another, but our souls do."

Meara looked at Jenny, who appeared to only be napping on the chaise, despite the words flowing from her mouth. *Such a beautiful, wise soul,* Meara thought. *Such an old soul.* "That's beautiful," she told Jenny's Higher Self.

"It is the truth."

"So Jenny learned from Adala's lifetime that humans are capable of great hatred, but in equal—if not greater—capacity the same amount of love. And from Menodora's lifetime Jenny is to learn..."

"That love knows no time or bounds. Unconditional love is timeless. We cannot create nor take from it. It simply is. It is the ultimate essence of all that we are."

"Jenny indicated before our session that she was interested in understanding the ripple effects of her actions, that she wanted help in seeing the bigger picture. Do you have anything that could help her better understand this?" Meara knew that the Higher Self was beginning to drift away. The regressions and past life experiences drew a lot of energy. It was an exhausting process for all who were involved.

"Choice."

"Choice?"

"Yes. She will understand better the next time. But for now, her understanding of love is the most important piece to the puzzle that she's trying to solve."

"Thank you. I will bring her back to the present now." Meara closed her notebook and set it on the small table beside her chair. In a gentle voice she recited the words that would bring Jenny back to her own time. "I will count down from ten and with each number you will become more aware of your present life and your current surroundings. Ten, you are leaving your other life behind..."

∞

Jenny felt tired after the session. Not just need-a-nap-tired, but run down and drained tired, as if she was the one who had ran and swam away from the fiery volcano. In a way, she supposed, she was. Even though it was a rare sunny day in Northeast Ohio, she had the curtains drawn. Caddie—who laid curled up on the couch—looked at her curiously, concerned at the strange behavior. Jenny shuffled over and scratched her furbaby behind the ears.

"It's ok, Caddie. I just feel drained." She hadn't listened to the recording yet, even though Meara had emailed it to her the next day. She shuffled around the tiny kitchen in her to-the-knee, boot style slippers, complete with pom-pom ties. Her mother liked to call them *obnoxious*. The scent of chai tea filled the air and Jenny placed the box of tea bags back inside the cabinet. She leaned against the counter, waiting for her favorite comfort drink to finish brewing.

The image of the erupting volcano was still vivid in her mind—three days later. She tossed and turned at night as she dreamed of the ash-covered world, her father stumbling and her mother's terrified eyes. Her mother. She'd ignored her call the other day. Well, she didn't hit the ignore button, she just let it go to voicemail. If she'd hit the ignore button right away, her mother would know that's what she'd done and ask even more questions. Sophia's pale blue eyes filled Jenny's mind as she rubbed her forehead. They'd seemed to have gotten along okay, Sophia and Menodora. Except.

Except Sophia didn't seem to realize Menodora's reservations about marrying Nikomedes. However, she did seem excited for the wedding itself: the dress, the processional, all of those sorts of details. But did she want

Menodora married off so badly, that she failed to see the type of person Nikomedes was? The kind of person that disappeared when something bad happened. Jenny snorted out loud as she carried her mug of tea to the bench window seat in the living room. She parted the curtain to let a sliver of sunlight through. Caddie curled up on the carpet in the center of the pool of light, enjoying its warmth.

Her phone buzzed and she glanced down. A text from Hadley, but even that couldn't snap her out of her thoughts. She'd call her in a little bit. She may not be able to keep promises to herself, but if it was a promise to someone else, Jenny was good for her word. Her phone buzzed a second time. This time the email icon popped up. Jenny picked up her phone, but it was only a message letting her know an author she enjoyed had a new book coming out. She made a mental note to add it to her Amazon shopping cart. Meara's email was marked as read, but still sitting in her inbox. Waiting. She was about to set her phone down when another message caught her eye.

Kevin Foley. With her regression appointments, she'd nearly forgotten about the email. It was at least two weeks old. This time, however, her stomach didn't do a somersault when she noticed it. In fact, besides sheer curiosity, there wasn't much of any other feeling there. That surprised her. Kevin had been in and out of her thoughts for the last year. And yet, she'd never felt inclined to contact him. Well, maybe in the beginning there was a couple of times she'd constructed a text message only to delete it before sending it. It just never felt right.

*It never felt right.* Jenny's eyes grew wide and she set the mug of tea down on the bench beside her. Just like Adala and Krischen. Just like Menodora and Nikomedes it never felt right. But with Evert, she'd known. Felt it almost instantly. Adala's soul had recognized Evert's soul and the deep connection, just as Menodora and Pleagia's souls recognized their sisterly bond. A memory came flooding back—not Adalas' or Mendora's—one of her own. An art exhibit. About a year and a half ago. Several of Jenny's pieces were being showcased in an exhibit at a small, private museum. She'd been beyond excited at the invitation, Hadley had even helped her choose which pieces to put into the exclusive collection. There was even going to be a write-up in *The Plain Dealer* about the featured artists. If she was really lucky, the curator would purchase one of her paintings, and if she was just plain lucky a patron would purchase one. The exposure was more than she could ask for, even if it didn't pay the bills at the time. It could pay off in dividends. She'd even splurged on a new dress from her favorite boutique.

Just as she was finishing her makeup, Kevin had called. His friend from college—in Akron—had called with tickets to one of the Elite Eight basketball games that night. And they were floor seats that he couldn't pass up. She understood, right? She remembered the cheering of the crowd in the background. Did it matter if she said yes, that she did mind? If he was already there? *Sure, no problem!* She'd even smiled into the phone. When she hung up, she immediately called Hadley, about to burst into tears and explained what happened. Thirty minutes later Hadley showed up in her best LBD and over-the-top costume jewelry ready to take the art exhibit by storm. That night, a patron had even commissioned a painting from her. Afterward, Hadley and she had gone out for drinks to celebrate.

And that night she hadn't cried. She didn't shed one single tear over the betrayal. Because deep down she knew. Maybe she had always known. She didn't open the message, instead she swiped her finger to the right and deleted if from her inbox.

# Chapter Nineteen

Hadley looked at Jenny in disbelief, which was rather impressive considering she was in downward-facing dog. They were in Hadley's yoga studio before it opened. The lights were off because the line of windows were streaming in the much welcome sunlight, creating rectangular patches across the floor. There were several candles on the window ledges, filling the room with earthy scents: sage, patchouli, lavender, and vanilla. Yoga wasn't necessarily Jenny's favorite activity, but Hadley's yoga studio was still one of her favorite places to be, besides her own art studio. Hadley's boyfriend, Jedd, often joked that Jenny created art with paint and canvas while Hadley created art with bodies and yoga mats.

Watching her friend twist and bend in the serene studio setting only deepened the notion that Jedd was right.

"I deleted it."

Hadley kicked her legs up, landing in a handstand. "Without even reading it?"

"Yup."

After a moment Hadley returned to a downward dog, then folded in her knees, coming to a hero pose, her butt on the mat and a bent leg on either side. "You weren't even a little bit curious?"

"I was, but this regression thing…it's really making me think."

Hadley smirked. "Past lives will do that to you."

"I mean, like, really think. About the choices I've made and the patterns of my lives, and of who I travel through these lives with." Jenny was seated cross legged on a mat across from Hadley. She picked at the mat's edge. "Take Adala. She married someone she barely knew just for the sake of being married. Only to find her true love after the fact. And Menodora, she was going to marry Nikomedes, except he was a total jerk face. I don't want that to happen to me."

Hadley moved her legs, so that they were stretched out in front of her. She had to limber up before the schedule of classes started, even though she'd been taking yoga for half her life and was more flexible than women half her age. "If you make a conscious effort, you can break the pattern. Like me. I learned the pattern of failure I had created in my other lives. And I made a conscious effort to choose differently this time." She gestured at the surrounding room. Her smile was both proud and peaceful.

"Did you learn anything else in your lives?" Jenny had never really asked Hadley for any of the details of her regression sessions. It seemed too invasive, almost like the violation of something sacred. But now she felt as though they shared this common bond, not only of the regressions, but of knowing that their lives were inextricably intertwined through centuries—millennia even—of friendship and sisterhood.

A thoughtful expression came over Hadley's face as she sat upright, folding her legs so that she was seated like a mermaid. "I did. I learned about friendship and about sacrifice. I learned that no matter what you may think, it's never too late."

Jenny sighed. "Tell that to my mom."

"You'll find the right guy, I promise. And when you do everything will fall into place. Including your mother."

"She picked Nikomedes as a husband for her Menodora! I wouldn't be surprised if she'd arranged for Adala to marry Krischen too!"

"It's possible. But your mom—as I'm sure Sophia did too—only has your best interest at heart."

Jenny stood up and carefully rolled up her mat. "That's easy for you to say. She isn't your mother!"

Hadley stood up and moved her own mat to the front of the classroom. She hit a few buttons on her cell phone and soft, instrumental music filled the studio. "Maybe this is her lifetime to break the pattern. Besides, she just wants what's best for you."

"Somehow I don't think setting me up with Cynthia-from-the-bank's recently divorced son with three kids is in my best interest."

"Maybe you should try online dating again." Hadley had met Jedd on one of those online dating sites, despite Jenny's unsuccessful attempts. She felt awkward talking to the barista at the Starbucks, let alone a complete stranger who she was supposed to be on a date with.

"If that's the only other option, I think I'd rather have my mother set me up."

Hadley grinned. "Careful what you wish for."

∞

Jenny turned onto the tree lined street where the house she grew up in was located. Her parents had lived in the house since she was three years old. Whereas, Jenny lived in a suburb on the outskirts of downtown Cleveland, her parents lived a bit further out from the city center. The houses were farther apart and they all had multi-car attached garages. Yards were well-kept and lavishly landscaped. She pulled up to the curb of the yellow, Cape Cod style house with its large, white front porch. It was nearing spring—as near to spring as it got in Northeast Ohio where the weather was notorious for seemingly going straight from winter into summer with barely a transition—and her mother's daffodils and hyacinth were starting to burst through the soil. The house had white trim and two white rocking chairs that sat on the porch. There was a Weeping Cherry Tree in the front yard that was currently blooming a pale pink.

The neighborhood was fairly cookie cutter, but it still felt like home. Not that her apartment didn't feel like home. Just coming *home-home* always felt different for some reason. She never could quite place her finger on it. Her mother had called, complaining about how she never sees her only daughter who only lives twenty minutes away. Other mothers got to spend time with their daughters, why didn't her daughter care enough to spend time with her? She wasn't getting any younger, you know, and before Jenny knew it, it would be too late and she'd be six feet under. Try spending time with her then! Finally, Jenny had conceded to coming over for dinner. It was a Saturday night and it wasn't like she had better plans at this point.

Jenny put her 2013 Chrysler Sebring in park. She got out and took a deep breath, clicking the lock button on the key fob. Truthfully, her car would be perfectly fine in this neighborhood, but it was habit. She walked across the tree lawn to the sidewalk then up the walkway leading to the front porch. It was just starting to get dark and the front lights weren't on. Her parents were expecting her, so she didn't bother knocking, instead she opened the screen door and pushed the heavy inside door—which was decorated with a paper flower and burlap wreath—open.

"Hello?" She called. The smell of her mother's Chanel perfume and pasta sauce filled the house. Her family wasn't Italian, in fact her father liked to joke they were simply American, a hodgepodge of different ethnicities that had blended into what was essentially a number of Western European cultures. She could hear a golf announcer in the background, her father was probably watching one of the PGA tournaments. Jenny was actually pretty good at golf herself, she had a great long game and a less than average short game, but she hadn't played in years.

"In the kitchen!" Her mother called, her voice drifting down the hallway to the foyer. Jenny sat her purse and keys on a small table near the door and slipped off her coat, hanging it on a hook. Her mother was extremely organized, a trait Jenny herself hadn't picked up.

She made her way down the hallway, past the framed photos of her progressing from kindergarten up through a senior in high school. It was almost like the hallway was a homage to Jenny's life. The sound of soft voices caught her attention and Jenny paused beside the bathroom doorway. No. No way. There was no way. She continued down the hallway and it ended at the open-concept kitchen, dining area, living space. Her mother was stirring sauce in a pot on the stove. In the living room, a beautiful green, sunshiny golf course played across the TV screen, only her father wasn't sitting on the couch watching it. Instead, he was already seated at the dining room table. Beside him were two other people. An older woman and a guy about Jenny's age. Neither of whom she recognized. Her father gave her an apologetic smile. Naturally, he'd probably tried to talk her mother out of it.

Her mother came over holding a wooden spoon, dripping sauce onto the countertop. "Jenny, this is Edna from my ceramics class. She told me all about her son, Gregory here—he's a *doctor*—and he just moved back to town from Idaho for a new position at one of the medical facilities in the area. I thought well, it would be proper to invite them over to dinner, so here we are!" She gave a slight giggle at the end which turned into a cough. "Why don't you have a seat and get to know each other?" She smiled, her dyed blonde curls bobbing on her head like little springs, before turning back to the stovetop.

Jenny forced a smile. This was not *spending time with her mother*. This was called manipulation. She pulled out the seat beside her father.

"Hello." It wasn't that she wasn't a friendly person, it was more that she was angry for being tricked. Even if it wasn't Edna's or Dr. Gregory's fault.

Edna smiled politely, but her son stuck his hand

out across the table. "Greg."

Jenny shook his hand. "Jenny."

"Well, then, uh…" her father stammered.

"Dinner sure smells good, Honey!" Mrs. McClain beamed.

"So you're a doctor?" Jenny asked, picking a piece of bread from the basket that her mother had already placed on the table.

"Yes, of ophthalmology." Greg nodded. He wasn't *bad* looking, Jenny decided. He had gray eyes and dark hair, with a five o'clock shadow. He wore glasses, but they made him look studious and sophisticated, as opposed to nerdy. He wore a navy colored sweater and a large gold wristwatch with a bright red face. Her mother could have chosen worse.

"So you like eyeballs?" Jenny didn't mean for it to come out crass sounding, but she was still annoyed at her mother. Her father practically spit his iced tea across the table and Edna gave out a nervous titter.

But Greg's face broke into a huge smile and he laughed. "Actually, yes. I find them fascinating."

Jenny's mind immediately went to her painting of Adala. She thoughtfully picked at her piece of bread. "Some would say the eyes are the windows to the soul."

Greg stopped laughing, but the smile remained. He had very straight teeth, but a small gap on one side. It was a perfectly, imperfect smile. He looked almost pensive. "They're more than windows, our eyes are as unique as our fingerprints—no pair is like any other—they aren't simply windows to the souls. To put it simply, they're a physical representation of all we are from our personality to our physical appearance to our emotional state. The eye is our window to the universe."

Jenny smiled—a genuine smile this time. Her mother was still rotten for setting the whole thing up without telling her about it, but maybe—just maybe—it wasn't going to be so bad after all.

# Chapter Twenty

The canvas stared back unblinkingly. Jenny knew she had to paint, she knew it as though she were being called to do it. It was relatively late by the time she'd gotten home, at least compared to the time she usually got home. It was well after 9 PM. Her usual routine would be to get into her pajamas and watch some Netflix with Caddie on the couch. But instead she'd slipped into a pair of torn jeans and a paint splotched t-shirt, prepared to be inspired.

She was in a good mood. She sort of hated to admit it. Her mom may have actually nailed it this time. Greg proved himself to be intelligent, funny, and charming—but not in a schmoozing, creepy kind of way—in a warm, genuine way. The doctor thing didn't impress her all that much. Sure, it was nice, but she'd always been more concerned with how someone treated other people, and from what she could tell Greg was kind and considerate.

The palette was on the stool next to the easel where she'd left it after painting Adala's eyes. That painting was now leaning against the windowsill. She hadn't told her mother, but when she shook Greg's hand good-bye, she'd slipped a tiny piece of paper with her phone number on it into his palm. She grabbed her MacBook from the other room and set it on the work table. She opened up her email and clicked on the message from Meara, the one containing the audio of her regression into the life of Menodora. Meara's voice filled the small room, counting Jenny down from the present back into the past. She began mixing colors, beautiful tropical hues. The images of Atlantis were still very fresh in her mind. If she closed her eyes she could almost hear the crash of the ocean waves and smell the salty air. The voices filled the empty spaces.

She began working somewhat methodically. Filling the canvas with a wash of colors: magenta, indigo, chartreuse. She kept adding it in layers until the desired affect was like a beautiful sunset. Then she set to work on the eyes. After her regression, she'd felt inspired, but time hadn't truly allowed her to get to the canvas until now. Caddie laid in a doggie bed that Jenny kept in her studio, curled up in a ball, her tail draped over her nose.

The eyes needed to be almost almond-shaped. Jenny closed her eyes remembering the reflection in the mirror: the long auburn curls and tan skin, the beautiful angular features that were somehow both strong and feminine at the same time. Almond-shaped eyes surrounded by lush, dark lashes and full eyebrows. Once she was satisfied with the shapes, she began mixing the iris color. The cerulean had to be just right, not too light, but not too dark—a perfect shade of blue like the exact color of where the sea would meet the sky.

She hoped Greg would call, but she couldn't force what wasn't meant to be. That's one of the things she'd learned without even realizing it. Adala's love for Krischen, it was forced, so it didn't work out. And Menodora's love for Nikomedes was an arranged marriage, again forced. Jenny huffed to herself, "We saw how that turned out, didn't we, Caddie?" Caddie opened one eye then went back to sleep. Jenny continued to mix different shades of blue. But the loves that weren't forced, like Adala and Evert, and the platonic love between

Pleagia and Menodora. Love—no matter its form—couldn't be forced. That's where she'd gone wrong with Kevin. She'd been trying to force love to happen where it wasn't meant to be.

"There! That's it!" She murmured excitedly, having found the perfect cerulean shade. In the background, Meara's voice was carefully guiding Jenny back to the present. "Not too light, and not too dark. Like the sky reflecting in the calmest of seas," Jenny said. She began to paint, carefully as not to rush the finishing touches. She added some soft white for highlighting, then took a few steps back. The familiar eyes of Menodora looked back at her. Jenny didn't feel as if she were painting from a dream. It felt more like she was painting from a memory. If the eyes really were the windows to the soul, were there similarities between Menodora's and Adala's eyes—even her own?

She set the newest painting down beside the older one, moved her easel out of the way and pulled the stool toward the middle of the room. She sat on it and stared at each painting. They were good. Better than she'd painted in a long time. And something was different. Not only were they not landscapes, but there was something else that had changed. The rawness—the eyes that looked back at her and the choices of the colors, allowed for a realness, a glimpse into Jenny's own authenticity that her previous paintings had been lacking. She studied the two pairs of eyes. What did she see there?

Resilience. Strength. Intelligence. Compassion. Love. A limitless amount of love that seemed to emanate from the canvas. Greg had said that a person's eyes were the windows to the universe. If that were true, Jenny realized, then the universe was a place abundant with love. Love without conditions. As soon as you put conditions on it, she thought, that's when everything changes. Unconditional love was the kind that stuck with you through multiple lifetimes.

"Now, open your eyes," Meara's voice said and then the recording ended.

∞

"So, wait." Hadley took a sip of her triple venti, nonfat, sugar-free vanilla, extra caramel, caramel macchiato. She wiped at the foam mustache across her upper lip with the back of her hand. "He was actually, like, normal? No second head? Or weird tics like burping repeatedly?"

Jenny shook her head. "Nope. He seemed perfectly normal. Nice, even."

"Wow. Your mom must not have met him beforehand."

Jenny smiled and took a sip of her own soy chai latte. That was probably true. Her mother always tried to set her up with the strangest men. Jenny had seen everything from men a good six inches shorter than her to the one Hadley had just referred—a poor guy who lived with his elderly aunt, her six cats, and who also had the unfortunate luck of a tic that caused him to burp about every thirty seconds. Loudly. And juicily. Jenny shuddered at the memory.

"I don't think she did."

"That's good. So tell me about this Gregory." Hadley leaned in excitedly. She was a big advocate for partaking in other people's happiness, joy was something to be shared she said.

"Well, he's a doctor. An ophthalmologist."

"An ophthalmologist is still a doctor. At least he's not a gynecologist." Leave it to Hadley to find the most inappropriate of comparisons.

"I'm not sure of his exact age, but he's probably thirty-four or so. He's smart, really funny, and sweet."

"What's he look like?"

"Gray eyes, dark hair, tall. Kind of rugged, I

guess. But also kind of geeky. Like a lumberjack who went to med school."

Hadley laughed. "Sounds perfect." She took another sip of her caramel macchiato. "Do you think he'll call you?"

Jenny shrugged. "It's already been two days. But I hope he will. If not…"

"If not, he's a damned fool." She picked up her cardboard cup and grabbed Jenny's wrist, making her mimic the same gesture. "To possibility!" She exclaimed and they clinked the cardboard cups together.

"To possibility," Jenny said with a hopeful smile.

# Chapter Twenty-One

The elevator seemed to zoom up to the twelfth floor faster than usual. Either that or she was used to coming to Meara's office now. *Third time's a charm.* The first time Jenny had come here she had been apprehensive, but now she felt the trill of excitement in her belly as she stepped out of the elevator and the doors closed behind her. She made her way down the hallway to Meara's office.

Just like the last two visits, the door was unlocked and Jenny slipped in, immediately helping herself to some tea. "Hello, Jenny!" Meara called from one of the back rooms.

"Hi, Meara! Did you want me to make you some tea?" Jenny called back.

"Yes, just some oolong, if you don't mind."

Jenny reached for another mug and began preparing the second cup of tea. It was all different now, yet it had only been in the span of a few weeks. Meara used to seem like a strange, untouchable spiritualist with her talk of other lives and the Higher Self, but now those things felt as natural to Jenny as the sky being blue. In a way it was as if she was awakening…to what exactly she wasn't sure. The truth? To life? Maybe to all of the above.

Meara came in from the back hallway. Today she was wearing a plum-colored tunic sweater with a chiffon ruffled hem over black leggings. Her auburn hair was in a haphazard pile on top of her head and it somehow made her appear younger. She came over and gave Jenny a side hug then gestured for her to sit in one of the chairs.

"How have you been since our last session?"

The answer came without thought. "Lighter."

"Lighter?" Meara took a sip of the steaming tea.

"Lighter, freer. It's as if experiencing Menodora's life opened something inside of me. Adala's life may have begun to chisel at it, but now I feel as if it's been completely blown wide open."

"In your heart space?"

Jenny nodded.

"Well, that's good." She looked thoughtful for a moment and took another sip of tea. "The lessons your soul has been learning have been powerful ones. You have a very advanced soul, Jenny. If I believed in such an abstract idea as luck, I'd say you were lucky."

"Luck doesn't even begin to describe it." Jenny set down the mug of tea, eager to begin the session, but not wanting to appear rude. She knew this part of the session was to help Meara understand the progress she was making, not simply a formality.

"Have you begun to notice the so-called butterfly effect of your life?"

"Actually, I think I have. Adala's selfless choice, allowed Keren to live a fulfilling life. And Pleagia—who is also Keren—her selflessness and loyalty to Menodora is what could have saved them."

"The regression ended before you explained whether they lived or perished," Meara pointed out.

"We all continue to live, regardless," Jenny replied slowly. It was a very not-Jenny response. And yet, she knew it to be truer than almost anything she'd ever felt before.

Meara's brown eyes were soft and she put a

hand over Jenny's. "That's exactly right. I think you're ready. Shall we begin today's session?"

∞

The boat was noisy. Ten-year-old Erin was less than pleased. She clung to the railing, white knuckled searching for the famed Statue of Liberty that would let her know they were near their destination. Her mother, father, and little brother Raffe—née Rafferty—were headed to America, the land of opportunity as her father liked to call it. Her red wool skirt was itchy and her knee socks kept sliding down. To top it off she'd scuffed her new Mary-Janes when they'd gotten onto the boat. She felt dirty, tired, and a bit nauseas. They'd been on the boat for ten days now. Initially she'd thought it wonderful, like an adventure out of one of the many books she loved to read. But then after several days, once the routine was established, the novelty had worn off.

Raffe came beside her, too short to see over the railing, although his curious blue eyes could peer between the rails. "Are we there yet?"

"All I see is water," Erin replied. It was windy too, her mother had made her strap her hat beneath her chin and she felt like a baby.

"Will we be there soon?"

"Isn't there someone else you can bother?" Erin snapped. Raffe's bottom lip quivered. He was a bit on the oversensitive side, but he was only six. Erin softened. "I'll let you know when I see something, okay?" Raffe nodded, satisfied, and ran off to find one of the many playmates he'd befriended during the long journey.

The sky was overcast, the sun hidden behind clouds. Erin knew they were getting close because the ship had slowed down its speed. Boats always did that before arriving at port, or so she'd read. Her stomach quelled with excitement. She was happy to go to America, she'd seen the pictures of the smiling women with their short, curly haircuts. She ran her hand down her own long, pigtail braid. Someday she'd have a fashionable haircut like that too. And yet, there was a lingering sadness in the pit of her stomach. She knew it was for the best, and not just because her father said it was so. The War of Independence was brutal and, like her mother said, it wasn't a good place to be raising two young children. Her father's cousin had moved to America ten years ago and was doing well working in construction and his wife was a teacher. Some girls thought it glamourous to be a model; Erin thought being a teacher was glamourous.

She'd miss her homeland's magnificent beauty though, with its rolling green hillsides and beautiful, cobalt blue seas. The air was always crisp and the lavender in her mother's garden always stood out brilliantly against the landscape. Then she saw it, pulling her back to the present. Looming in the distance was the tallest statue she'd ever seen. A pale green woman, with a torch held high in her right hand and a funny looking crown on her head. She breathed in the salty air. *We're here!* She let go of the railing and ran to find Raffe.

# Chapter Twenty-Two

The building was crowded. Erin could hear the various languages—some guttural sounding and some like the trill of a song—coalescing into an echo in the massive space. And it smelled bad. Although, Erin was sure she didn't smell all that great herself. She was holding her small suitcase that contained all the belongings she could afford to take with her on the journey to America. She'd given over half her doll collection to her best friend, Siobhan. At least she knew they'd be in good hands. Raffe was getting whiney and antsy, anxious to get out into their new home and explore, but also irritated at having to wait in the never-ending lines.

While still on board the ship, they had received what Erin already knew to be one of two physical exams.

She had seen the letter from her father's cousin lying open on his desk one afternoon. Erin's suspicions were confirmed when they reached the top of the stairs and saw several examination stations. She noticed each man wearing a white coat—the doctor—was holding a piece of chalk, periodically using it to mark the clothes of the immigrant with something Erin couldn't see.

"What's he doing, Mother?" Erin whispered, surprised that her mother heard her soft-spoken words and that they weren't swallowed up by the loud, boisterous voices surrounding them.

"He's marking the people," Mother replied in her thick Irish-accented English. Erin's family could speak both Gaelic and English, which even at ten-years-old she knew would enable her father to get a good job and allow for her and Raffe to go to school.

"Why?" Raffe asked, having picked up on the conversation.

"For illnesses. They do not want people from the other countries to bring diseases to the New World. America wants strong people who are built to work."

"Are we strong, Mother?" Raffe asked. But instead of answering, she just squeezed his hand tighter.

They shuffled along the line, drawing closer to

the doctors with their chalk. Erin could hear broken English—translators—who accompanied those immigrants who could not speak the language of the New World. Erin's mind drifted back to home. She wondered what time it was and if Siobhan missed her, and if she was at least taking comfort in the dolls she'd left behind. Was school the same without her? Probably not, she decided. She was the smartest in her glass and Miss O'Connell loved her. Surely, she was being missed.

The line shuffled forward once more. From what Erin could tell the lines were organized by country of origin. She could hear the familiar, soft, lyrical sounds of her native tongue behind her, a small family of a man and woman with a baby. Surprisingly, the baby didn't cry despite the warmth, noise, and smell. As she turned to move forward, a young boy about her age in the line next to theirs caught her eye. He had blonde hair and round blue eyes that almost seemed too large for his face. He quickly looked away, then back at her again, giving her a tentative smile.

*"Heileo,"* Erin smiled, reverting to Gaelic.

The boy's grin widened. "Hallo."

She didn't recognize the language, then again she didn't know anything besides English and Gaelic. But she felt relieved. At least some words were obvious in any language. Before she could try and ask the boy where he was from, the line shuffled forward once more. The doctor stood before them, white chalk in hand. Her family was next.

∞

The doctor examined the children first. He listened to their lungs and hearts. Checked their ears, nose, eyes, and throat then did a quick once over of their scalps and skin, presumably looking for lice or rashes. But Erin wasn't worried. She knew that she and Rafferty were both healthy and strong. Her parents were too, if they weren't they wouldn't be able to work in America. And that was the whole point of coming in the first place. Avoid the War and create a new life. A new life required work. Erin also knew that if she weren't healthy, she wouldn't be able to attend school. That would be a nightmare, she'd decided, and was careful to avoid any one on the ship who coughed, sneezed, itched or otherwise looked sickly. She also was quite diligent in consuming fruits and vegetables as often as possible.

Raffe's hand was sweaty in her own as they waited for the doctor to continue his examination of their father. When the man was finished, he moved on to her mother, examining her quickly. If Erin had to guess the examination took no more than a minute or two. How anyone could surmise anything in such a short amount of time was beyond her. The doctor frowned and Erin felt her heart leap. He took the chalk and wrote a *Pg* on her mother's left shoulder, right on her brown, wool traveling coat. Yet, he didn't pull her aside, or send them off with someone else. Instead they started to make their way with the next surge of people.

Erin was still panicked—what did those letters mean? But before she could think about it, she heard a high-pitched wail from behind her. She turned. It was the same tow-headed boy with the big, blue eyes. Tears streamed down his face, even though he was much too old for such a display of uncontrollable emotion. The crowd tugged her along, and she craned her neck to watch the scene unfolding.

The doctor had marked something on the man—perhaps the boy's father—and the woman—his mother—was gesticulating wildly as tears streamed down her face. The man tried to calm her down. He moved slightly to comfort her, and Erin noticed the limp. He must have been marked with a deformity or illness indicator. Erin felt her heart wrench for the poor boy. The boy continued to sob as the man leaned over and tried to console him. The woman also held a toddler on her hip. Erin surmised that the marks were some sort of code. She knew that if it was something bad—like mental illness, deformity, or disease—that a person was considered unfit to work. The New World also had to keep the population as healthy as possible, especially with the influx of new people arriving daily. The man would be held up at Ellis Island for a more thorough examination—or worse—sent back to wherever he came from. He and his wife had to decide which children—if any—would stay behind.

The line stopped moving and Erin watched as the man talked to the woman. He said something and kissed her cheek. She nodded, brushing away her tears with her free hand. Then she took hold of the still-crying boy and, with the toddler still on her hip, she threw her shoulders back as best she could and moved into the surge of people headed for Interrogation.

∞

This room was not much better. There were long tables and workers with interpreters sat at them, verifying names of immigrants with the ship records. The line began moving faster now. Erin felt her stomach grumble. She hadn't eaten since breakfast and she had no idea what time it was. Raffe's wide-eyed wonder had vanished replaced with a lackluster look that was a combination of hunger and sleep-deprivation.

They reached the table and the man looked at the ship records asking their father to verify the names of his wife and children, their ages, where they came from, and their religious affiliation. Her father answered all of the questions. The man nodded then stamped two sets of papers, handing one to her father. Her father picked up Raffe, who was falling asleep on his feet, and Erin was happy to be relieved of her duty as caretaker for a while. Before they walked away to go fetch the rest of their luggage the interpreter—who was female—smiled at their mother.

"Congratulations," she said in English.

"Thank you," their mother replied in English equally as good. Perhaps, their mother could work as an interpreter. That would be an interesting job, Erin thought. She didn't think twice about the congratulations, assuming the woman was congratulating them on their successful entry into America.

She followed close behind her parents as they followed the next line of people surging forward to retrieve luggage. She also knew that they would have to exchange their Irish currency for American currency before they would take the ferry over to the mainland. After reaching the mainland, they'd stay at her father's cousin's house until they could find a place of their own. It would be cramped quarters, as the cousin had a wife and three children of his own, but they would make do. Maybe it would even be fun, Erin thought, to meet some children around her own age.

As they waited for Father to retrieve the rest of their luggage from the ship, Mother held Raffe, even though he was much too big to be held anymore. He was sound asleep on her left shoulder, and that's when Erin remembered the *Pg,* which was already smudged and fading from her mother's coat.

"Mother?" she asked. "What were those letters the doctor marked on your shoulder? I know that you are well, otherwise, you would not have been able to pass through."

"I should have told you sooner, darling, but I was afraid that you would be worried during our journey. But now that we are here in America, ready to begin our new lives, it is a good time to tell you that we also will be having a new addition to our family." Her tired face broke into a toothy smile, she rubbed at her stomach with her right hand, smoothing the folds of her coat and flower-printed dress.

"Wait—you're pregnant?" Erin was shocked. How had she not noticed? But her shock quickly turned to excitement. "When?"

"Five more months."

"And Father?"

"He knows, of course. We haven't yet told your father's cousin, but we hope that we will have our own living arrangements by the time the baby arrives."

Erin felt her face flush with excitement. Her father returned with a cart stacked with their luggage. She didn't hear as he discussed with Mother where they needed to go in order to catch the ferry. A new brother or sister. A new house and a new school in a new country. It really was a new life. A new, wonderful life that was full of surprises.

# Chapter Twenty-Three

The umbrella wasn't doing much to protect her from the rain. Rain in Cleveland was never attractive, especially in the spring. It was almost like the sky was angry and punishing the people below. Erin had thought spring was supposed to be pretty—brightly colored flowers, little green blades of grass, birds singing. But not in Cleveland. The lake made sure the springtime was cold and rainy.

Erin craned her neck to see if there were any cabs headed in her direction. Cars drove by splashing water onto the curb soaking her t-strapped heels. She just wanted to hail a cab, get out of the rain and over to the library where she could bury her head in some books. Reading was something she did not have the luxury of doing at home. Between Rafferty and Fiona's constant arguing, there was little peace to be had. It was difficult being the eldest and having to help take care of her two little siblings—the youngest of which was a good ten years younger. Some of her other friends had already married, but Erin hadn't met anyone who impressed her yet, much to her parents' disdain.

They'd been in America for ten years—Fiona being the only member of the family who was born an American citizen. Her father had found work for Carnegie's steel industry. Her mother worked as a seamstress out of the home, her primary responsibility being the children whenever they weren't in school. Erin wasn't simply going to the library for pleasure—it was also where she worked, and if a cab didn't show up soon, she was going to be late.

The rain began to pick up and Erin noticed headlights swinging in her direction. Finally! She waved her free hand and the cab slowed, sliding up to the curb. Erin yanked open the door, awkwardly shaking out the umbrella, but thankful to be out of the rain. As she shut the door, she smoothed water droplets off her jacket and said, "The library on Superior." At the same time a deep, male voice said, "The Arcade." Erin turned toward the voice.

A young man, about twenty-years-old had entered the same cab from the other side. His shoulders were wet and he was wearing a hat. Hearing the female voice, he turned toward her, his eyes were large and blue in his angular face. Erin had a moment of recognition, but it quickly disappeared. She knew one thing, she was not the one who was going to get back out into the rain. The cab driver peered at them in the rear view mirror.

"So which is it? The library or the Arcade?" His voice was raspy from one too many smoked cigarettes.

"The library."

"The Arcade." The man's cheeks reddened. "I mean, if you don't mind, we can drop the lady off at the library first, then take me on to the Arcade?"

"Sure. This rain is making traffic a bit difficult. A little rain and suddenly no one knows how to drive around here," the driver grumbled, more to himself than to his passengers.

"Sorry about that. I hope you don't mind sharing the ride?" The young man asked. He took off his hat, revealing neatly-coifed blonde hair, and placed it on his knee.

Erin felt her cheeks flush even though she wasn't

sure why. She absent-mindedly ran her hand over her own chin-length hair. "Oh. Well, of course not. I mean, it is raining after all."

An awkward silence passed between them, then at the same time as Erin said, "This weather is horrendous." The man said, "Spring time in Cleveland." They both chuckled. Another silence passed, but this one slightly more comfortable than the last. Erin looked away, out the rain-streaked window, but found herself drawn back to the man sitting beside her, his blue eyes like a beacon despite the overcast day.

"So, do you work at the Arcade?" she asked, unable to stop herself. Her parents were forever scolding her for her inquisitive nature, despite the political and social changes occurring all around them, they were still traditional in the most annoying of ways.

The man didn't seem to mind though. "Indeed, I do. I work with numbers, but I have a feeling that wouldn't interest you."

Erin was surprised he was already making assumptions and they'd only just met. Well, sort of met. "And how would you know that?" The traffic was stop-and-go as they were carted around the city.

"You said you were headed to the library, didn't

you?"

"I did."

"You look like a modern woman, so I assume it would be safe to say you work at the library; therefore, your preference is probably words to numbers." His blue eyes were intense and it made Erin's heart beat harder in her chest. Who was this strange man? And of all the people in the city, how was it that she was sharing a cab with him?

"In fact, I am and I do. I also prefer books to people." She said in a clipped tone, leveling him with a steady gaze. Instead of recoiling from her verbal jab, he laughed, a deep, appreciative laugh.

Then he surprised her by extending his hand and saying, "I'm Patrick."

Erin shook his hand. "Erin."

She smiled despite herself.

∞

The stacks of books provided comfort to Erin. She basked in the silence of the written word and the smell of centuries old paper, ink, and leather. The rain pelted the window pane and she pushed her little metal cart up and down the aisles. One of her responsibilities was to re-shelve books that had been returned. A lover of books and a voracious reader, she also found comfort in the predictability of the Dewey Decimal System. See, Patrick was wrong. She *did* like numbers. Her brain liked order, most likely the result of her boisterous and erratic younger siblings.

The hushed whispers of the patrons provided a soft background music. The cart's left back wheel squeaked slightly as she pushed it along, periodically stopping to return a book to its rightful place on the shelf. Occasionally, Erin would stop and pick up a book, rifling through its pages, even stopping to read a few chapters. She was supposed to shelf one cart every ninety minutes, but she was very quick. She'd been working at the library since she was sixteen. Most of the aisles were as well-known to her as the back of her own hand. Her favorite section was the mystery section, tucked away within the 800s.

She didn't hear the footsteps behind her. She leaned against the shelf, biting at her thumbnail, smudging her fire engine red lipstick. He cleared his throat. Startled she dropped the book. It bounced off the metal cart—sounding like a gunshot in the silence of the library—and hit the floor with a thud. Standing before her wearing a bashful expression was the young man from the taxi ride.

Erin covered her heart with her hand and noticed it was pounding in her chest. Was it pounding from the scare or from seeing Patrick standing there, his coat dripping wet from the rain and forming a small puddle at his feet. Finally, she caught her breath.

"You scared me nearly half to death. You shouldn't sneak up on someone like that!" she scolded.

He gave her an apologetic grin. "I thought I'd come check out a book."

She bent over and picked up the book, returning it to its home on the shelf without even looking. "Shouldn't you be at work?"

"It's my lunch break."

"Already?"

"It's well past eleven."

Erin began to push the mostly empty cart down the aisle. Her heart was finally returning to a semi-normal rhythm. "What kind of book are you looking for?"

"What do you recommend?"

"Oh, the classics, Mark Twain, Shakespeare, the Brontë sisters. Personally, I love a good mystery, you know, Sherlock Holmes."

"Really? I would have pegged you for a

romantic."

Erin snorted. "Hardly. Where's the intellectual challenge in a romance novel?" She pushed the cart back to the main area where the latest books were displayed on a table.

"You like a challenge then?"

"I do." She paused, turning to look at him. His eyes were sparkling and she suspected he was up to something. And that it didn't have to do with checking out books.

"Then I challenge you to a cycling race."

"Now?"

"Of course not."

"When?"

"Whenever you want." He lowered his voice which had begun to rise in excitement. "The sooner the better."

"Where?"

"The park near the lake. The one that rents bicycles."

She wasn't sure why she was indulging him. He was a complete stranger to her. They'd only shared a cab ride and it had only lasted all of ten minutes. And yet, here he was standing in front of her wearing a mischievous grin. It was either a magnificent idea or it was a downright crazy one.

"I don't work tomorrow afternoon."

"Great. About one o'clock then?"

She found herself nodding. Patrick's grin grew into a full-blown smile. He began to walk backward, toward the library's main doors, tripping over a table leg at the end of the aisle and knocking over several books. Erin rushed to pick them up and a couple other patrons stopped to help. She thanked them and when she stood up, books pressed to her chest, Patrick had already disappeared back into the rainy Cleveland morning.

∞

The wind whipped off the lake. It wasn't the most ideal day for a bicycle ride, but the sun was shining and the air was warm against her skin. She supposed she couldn't complain. She'd had her doubts about coming today—the man was a total stranger, he could be a thief or worse a murderer—and yet she found herself getting dressed and hailing a cab to the bicycle rental station. It was as if her heart was operating separately from her mind. It both confused and exhilarated her.

She pulled her sweater tighter around her waist and that's when she saw the tall, lanky form come into view. His blonde hair ruffled by the wind. Something was slung over his arm and it wasn't until he was several feet away that she noticed it was a picnic basket.

"Good afternoon!" he smiled.

"I thought we were having a proper bicycle race?" she teased.

"We are. Only I thought you might be hungry so I stopped on the way and picked up a few things." He said, nodding at the picnic basket. He started walking toward the rocky shore of Lake Erie, on the other side of the bicycle path. Setting down the basket, he pulled out a blanket inviting her to sit down.

"Don't think this gets you off the hook," Erin smiled. She couldn't believe someone would go to all this trouble simply to take her on a date. Not to mention, one of the better dates she'd ever been on. At least so far.

"Oh, I don't doubt it." He pulled out a baguette, some cheese, sparkling grape juice, and prosciutto, setting it down on the blanket between them. "I don't want to be totally humiliated when I lose the race. If anything I was hoping this might slow you down."

Erin laughed and popped a chunk of cheese into her mouth. Maybe—just this once—she'd let someone else win.

# Chapter Twenty-Four

It was several months later when Erin and Patrick returned to the park where they'd had their first date. It was the sweltering days of summer in Cleveland, Ohio. The air felt as though it were pressing in on you from all sides, like a heavy weight was tied to each breath. The humidity was stifling and just laying beneath the Buckeye tree's shade didn't do much to protect them from the sun's unrelenting heat.

Erin rested her head in Patrick's lap, his back pressed against the solidity of the Buckeye's trunk. It was too hot to ride bicycles, and even the usual whoops of excitement from the nearby beachfront were silent on this particular day—not very refreshing when the water isn't that much cooler than the air itself. These were the dog days of summer, as Erin's mother liked to say. Labor Day was fast approaching and with it increased hours at the library, so Patrick and Erin had taken full advantage of the time they could spend together. Today they'd settled on reading books in the park, but in the sweltering heat, their fingers seemed to stick to the pages, as if the books themselves also thought it was much too hot and humid to do the work of being read. Patrick was reading some book by a newer author named Sinclair Lewis, while Erin was reading one of her favorites, *Wuthering Heights,* for the umpteenth time when she sighed and snapped the book closed. Not only was the weather stifling, but there was something else that had been bothering her. About Patrick.

It wasn't necessarily something bad. More like an inkling. They'd been seeing one another exclusively for a few months now. They'd met each other's families and Erin was surprised that when he encountered the chaos of her household he didn't go running for the hills. In fact he had seemed amused. His family had been pleasant as well. His mother was soft-spoken and her English was a bit broken with her native tongue being German. He also had a younger brother, Henry, who was quite mischievous and in his early teen years, a couple years younger than

Raffe. His father too was very kind, yet there was a certain dignity about him, a sort of strength. Patrick's father worked in a brewery and his mother was very involved in their church. And yet, despite the apparent normalcy, something had struck her. His mother, Louisa, is the one who stuck in Erin's mind long after their first meeting.

Not that they'd spent much time together, but on the rare afternoons, Erin would try to engage the petite woman in conversation and she would do her best to answer in her limited English. She had a basic knowledge, and Erin would have been happy to tutor her for free, but felt that the offer could be misinterpreted as demeaning. But it was her eyes that haunted—no, haunted wasn't the right word—taunted her. Louisa had large, soft blue eyes that seemed to sparkle at the centers, but a sort of dullness had begun to creep in. She often wore her pale blonde hair swept up, revealing the sharp features of her heart-shaped face. But the eyes seemed...as though Erin had seen them in a dream. Only, she knew it wasn't in a dream, she was sure of it. She just couldn't place where she knew those eyes from, but she was one hundred percent certain she had seen those imploring eyes once before.

"Have you lived here your entire life?" Erin finally asked, plucking some blades of the cool grass from the ground beside her and feeling the warmth of Patrick's body cradling her head.

"Hmmm?" Patrick barely looked up from his book.

"Have you always lived in Cleveland?"

Seeming slightly annoyed, but ever the exerciser of patience, Patrick reluctantly closed his book and set it on the grass beside him. He stroked a strand of hair away from her face, and looked down at her, a contemplative look on his face.

"No. We lived in Germany until I was about ten or so. Then my mother, Henry, and I lived in a tenement in New York City for a couple years with some other German immigrants. And then we moved to Lititz, Pennsylvania once my father immigrated. Initially, he'd been sent back to Germany due to a misunderstanding about his health. We'd hoped he'd be sent to some sort of holding place, but he was shipped—quite literally—all the way back to Germany. We didn't see him for two years. That was a difficult time. And then Father got the job offer in Cleveland, and well, here we are." He continued to absent-mindedly stroke Erin's hair as he spoke as if talking about it took him back in time.

Erin's story wasn't much different. They'd lived with her father's cousin in New York City for about a year, to earn some money, but city life was rough on her, Raffe, and Fiona, but especially their mother. It was too bustling, too busy, too noisy too everything. Her father had done some odd jobs, the ones no one else seemed to want to do, but eventually they'd saved enough money and moved to Pittsburgh, where her father found a job with Carnegie Steel. The family preferred the smallness of that city, but walking everywhere with all those crazy hills was not one of Erin's fonder memories. Eventually, her father was transferred to Cleveland and as part of the deal the family was given a small duplex in a suburb outside of the city. It was one of the reasons Erin couldn't wait to begin work—thank goodness it was becoming more acceptable for women to have jobs, much to her mother's dismay. But she was helping with the bills and even saving for the possibility of attending university. Truth be told she was pretty sure she would have shipped Raffe and Fiona back to Ireland herself if she hadn't gotten her job at the library downtown.

Suddenly, a memory came rushing back from the recesses of her mind. A memory from a decade ago when she and her family had first immigrated to America. The thousands of people pouring into Ellis Island. The registration and the medical exams. A smile shared with a young, tow-headed boy who had big, blue eyes. A man being told something in German and a young woman with a toddler on her hip, holding back her tears as she and the other little boy progressed through the immigration process, but the man did not. Erin sat up quickly, practically smacking Patrick in the chin with the top of her head.

"Hey, is everything okay?" Patrick asked, eyes concerned but words revealing his bewilderment.

"It was you."

"What was me?"

"In immigration. In line. Your father was marked during the medical examination. And I remember you standing there. You smiled at me. Henry was just a toddler and I remember them telling your family something in German. Your mom looked upset, but she proudly threw her shoulders back and progressed to the next stage, but your father didn't go. That was you."

"Are you sure?"

"I'm certain. Your mother's eyes. I could not forget eyes that held so much dignity, yet softness at the same time. Doesn't it make perfect sense? You've always felt so familiar to me."

Patrick shook his head at her like she was crazy.

"Tell me it isn't true." Erin pushed herself up so she was kneeling in front of Patrick, practically nose to nose. "Tell me that you don't feel it, too. That it seems as though we've always known one another."

Patrick tilted his head which Erin took as an affirmation of her words. She knew he felt it too, in the way he looked at her and in the gentleness of his touch. As if he had to handle her fragilely because at any moment she would disappear like a ghost, a whisper of a dream.

"You were there. I was there. We were both there. And you smiled at me. Just like you did in that taxicab."

"I'm sorry, Love. I believe you, but I don't remember that at all."

Erin wasn't deterred. "You were distracted. Your father was being sent back to Germany. Of course you wouldn't remember some little brown-haired, Irish girl in the line next to you." Erin paused. "That's when I found out my mother was pregnant with Fiona." And then she rushed on, seemingly unable to stop the rush of words.

"It's fate. What are the odds that we would randomly meet, nearly a decade later, in a taxicab in Cleveland, Ohio? One in a million? One in a billion?"

"You sound like you've been reading one too many of those romance novels you dislike."

Erin frowned. "You don't believe in fate."

Patrick bit his lip in thought, considering. "I believe in serendipity."

"Serendipity and fate are practically the same thing," Erin pointed out.

Patrick grabbed her hand rubbing his thumb gently back and forth across her knuckles. "Yes, but fate is such a heavy word, like there's no choice in the matter. Serendipity allows for the element of surprise."

"Fate, serendipity, whatever you want to call it, even if you want to call it magic, it's meant to be. We're meant to be." Erin smiled leaning in and kissing him softly on the lips.

"Well, I'm glad you feel that way because I've been thinking the same thing for about a month now." Patrick pulled back from the kiss and reached into his pants pocket.

"Yes! A million times over yes!" Erin threw her arms around his neck before he could even pull out the ring for which he'd been saving so prudently. Before he could even ask her the question for which he'd been practicing so diligently for over a month. Fate? Serendipity? The word didn't matter, but he knew it from the moment that he met her on that rainy day in the taxicab that Erin Murphy was a very special woman. If only he'd been able to know how special.

# Chapter Twenty-Five

The wedding was simple. They'd decided it would be best to wait until the weather cooled off, which made the end of September perfect. Fall in the Midwest was unlike anywhere else. The air was crisp and cool with a light breeze. Leaves were abloom with their various shades: gold, pumpkin, and scarlet. They settled on a vineyard setting a little further east than their hometown. They'd honeymoon in one of the bed and breakfasts before returning home to the Goebel's house, where they would live—a little less chaotic than the Murphy household—until they could find an apartment of their own near the city and both of their jobs. Also, nearer to the action. As a young married couple they wanted to take advantage of the parks, plays, and other activities that city life had to offer.

The vineyard was on a hill and Erin wore her mother's wedding dress, cheekily altered into a fringe and lace version that was indicative of the times. Erin had insisted on keeping it fairly casual. She insisted that Patrick wear what made him feel most comfortable, and not wanting to be a total dolt, he settled on a light gray suit and indigo colored tie, Erin's favorite color as well as a match to the wine of the vineyard. Only their families were in the wedding party, each member wearing their best suit or dress, including Fiona, Raffe, and Henry. Close friends were invited, as well as family, but most of their families had either stayed in New York City, or migrated to cities like Boston, Pittsburgh, and Chicago and couldn't afford the fare or extravagance of attending a wedding in Ohio. A small handful of relatives who lived around the Cleveland and Youngstown area, were in attendance, and that didn't bother Erin none as her feelings about it were the simpler the better.

The vineyard owners had made an elaborate wood, ribbon, and flower canopy that was arranged so the wedding guests could see out into the vineyard. Patrick's hands were sweaty as they wrapped around Erin's smaller, daintier ones. The ring wasn't much, but Erin didn't mind that either. It wasn't the wedding or the ring or any of that frivolity that mattered to Erin. All that mattered to her was that she'd found her soulmate. She knew few people were so lucky—after watching the numerous obligational or arranged marriages around her—and she felt blessed beyond words to be so fortunate. Fate, serendipity, destiny. It didn't matter what it was, only that it *was.*

The priest looked at her, having asked the same questions he'd already asked of Patrick, and now expecting an answer. Erin smiled broadly, the light breeze tickling her neck and causing a loose strand of chestnut hair to fall near her ear.

"I do."

∞

It wasn't long before Erin was expecting. It temporarily put a damper on her plans for attending university, but she was anything but deterred. Thwarted maybe, but she knew that Patrick supported her dreams and if attending university is what Erin wanted, eventually attending university is what Erin would get.

It hadn't taken long before they found a small duplex just outside the city. The timing had been almost uncanny; they only stayed with the Goebel's for two weeks before one of Patrick's co-workers was looking for a tenant. Erin gazed out the small kitchen window that looked out onto the tiny, decaying garden of the neighboring house. She rubbed her belly affectionately, somehow now used to the foreign little human that had invaded her body. Pregnancy had always both horrified and fascinated her, but she had gotten used to the feeling quickly, as well as to the little punches and the little kicks. She was five months pregnant and it was February now.

The weather had been a bit atypical, mild for a Cleveland winter. One day it was forty degrees—another day had even reached sixty degrees—then the next day it would be back into the twenties and thirties. The snow was mild too, which slightly disappointed her. She secretly enjoyed the snow, but whenever she ran into a stranger who grumbled about it she'd amicably join in for the camaraderie. There was one day where there was almost half a foot of the white stuff, but once the temperature hit sixty degrees four days later, it was gone, the remaining puddles the only lingering evidence of the snow.

She'd cut back her hours at the library after her first trimester. A stack of books sat on the kitchen table, each bookmarked in various places, none completed. She'd taken a liking to decorating the nursery with a combination of trips to the department store with her mother and hand-me-downs from Fiona's and Raffe's childhoods. Sometimes while Patrick was at work she would go into the bright, yellow room with its little stuffed zoo animals and run her hand along the worn, wooden crib. Then she'd pull open the sheer curtains to make the room extra cheery. She would sit in the rocking chair—the same one that Mrs. Goebel had rocked both Patrick and Henry in when they were babies—the wood smooth from wear, just like the crib. She'd sit and rock, talking to the little human forming inside her, telling him—or her—about his mommy and daddy, who they were, where they were from and how they met. She'd speculate about her dreams for her child's future. The baby was due in May. Erin herself was only twenty-one, she could only imagine what her own child's life could be like twenty-one years from now. There could be flying cars and trips to Mars for all she knew! She always had had a vivid imagination. Sometimes she would read children's fairy tales and nursery rhymes to her bulging tummy, hoping that the baby would hear and adopt his parents' love of reading. Stories that were filled with both new beginnings and happy endings.

∞

Much to Patrick's protests, even at five months pregnant, Erin still insisted on going into the library twice a week. Her regular days were Tuesday and Thursday. It helped to break up the monotony of being home alone and the anticipation of the baby's arrival. Even though she wouldn't admit it, she also loved how the other librarians fawned over her growing pregnant belly and asked her about potential baby names. They both enjoyed somewhat traditional names: Michael if it was a boy and Emma if it was a girl.

*Four more months,* Erin thought as she pulled a felt wool hat down over her recently cropped, bobbed hair. She found her good wool coat and a knitted scarf from her mother, before grabbing her leather work satchel and heading out the door. The weather was gloomy on this particular day. The sky was gray and overcast, low-hanging clouds with bellies full of snow. The night before it had rained, turning into a slushy mix in the early morning before coating the world in droplets of ice as the temperature continued to drop. *Be careful,* Patrick had warned before kissing her on the forehead on the way out, it could be *slippy*. Erin smiled at the memory as she used the railing to guide herself carefully down the steps of the front porch. How quickly they'd fallen into the dialect of the Cleveland area, despite being immigrants. She'd already made arrangements with the taxi service to take her downtown to the library. In fact, she'd even lucked out and had the same fellow as her driver each time. His name was Marvin and he was probably in his sixties with a thick Scottish accent. Her own accent was all but gone after ten years in America, except of course when around family and friends from Ireland it was easy to slip back into the language of home—her faraway, almost a distant memory home. She hoped she wouldn't forget. She tried not to forget the rolling emerald hills contrasted against the cobalt blue sky, well, cobalt blue on a good day.

Just as she made it to the curb, Marvin's taxi came into view, ambling down the street before coming to a stop right at her feet. Ever the gentleman, Marvin jumped out of the driver's seat and helped her into the backseat, gently shutting the door behind her. The cab smelled of pipe smoke and leather, something else that sparked faint memories of her own grandfather, well into his nineties and still living back in Ireland with what family had stayed behind during the War. Marvin checked his mirrors before pulling away from the curb and heading toward the towering buildings of downtown Cleveland.

"How are you feeling, Mrs. Goebel?" He asked, deep blue eyes darting into the rearview mirror for the briefest of seconds before returning to the road. It wasn't a peak traffic time, although Erin was adamant about keeping a regular schedule of 10 AM- 3 PM. This allowed for her to leave just after Patrick and return just before him. It also allowed her to get in a nap before she began dinner preparations. The tiredness was reaching the point where some days it wore on her like a heavy cloak.

She smiled and gave the reply she always gave to Marvin. "Oh, the usual mix of excitement and sleepiness." She laughed and the sound was light-hearted with just a slight sense of weariness beneath it.

"Well, you look wonderful. Most beautiful pregnant woman I ever seen," Marvin replied. It was the same reply he gave her every Tuesday and Thursday. It was like some sort of dance between the two of them, a ritual of conversation.

"Why, thank you, Marvin. This weather is downright crazy. Six inches of snow one day and sixty degrees several days later. I have half a mind to move to

California." A light flurry of soft snowflakes tumbled from the sky.

"Now what would you do in California, Mrs. Goebel?" Marvin asked as he made the turn onto the main road. They were only about ten minutes from the library.

"Be an actress? Open a vineyard?"

"Well, you do have the looks to be an actress," he glanced at her again, "but do you have the skills to be believable in those fancy movie roles? Can you walk the walk and talk the talk?"

Erin chuckled. "My mother always said I had a flair for the dramatic."

Marvin chuckled too. "Somehow, I don't think that's quite the same thing."

Even though she dreamed of leaving Ohio for someplace warmer and more pleasant looking, she knew she would probably never leave. It would be difficult to leave both the Murphy's and the Goebel's behind. If anything, the sense of family was deeply instilled in both Erin and Patrick, an awareness of the sacrifices their parents had made in coming to America in order to ensure both of them a better future, a better future for their grandchildren.

The two sat in amicable silence as Marvin

carefully navigated the streets toward the library. Erin looked forward to the warm cup of tea she knew her friend, and fellow librarian, Milly, would already have prepared for her. Marvin pulled up right in front of the library, and put the taxi into park. He hurried over to Erin's door behind the passenger seat and pulled it open, offering her his arm. She took it and gently lifted herself out of the car, still getting used to the extra weight in her abdomen and how it threw off her sense of balance.

"Back here at 3 PM on the dot, Mrs. Goebel," Marvin assured her as he guided her around the front of the car and toward the curb.

"Thank—" she started to say just as her boot was about to hit the curb. A loud honk sounded and Erin turned.

Time seemed to slow down all around her. She watched as another taxicab hit a patch of black ice, causing the driver to lose control. The giant, yellow hood and black grill was barreling toward her, the driver unable to regain control. She felt Marvin try to pull her out of the way—it was either that or try to stand in between the careening car, possibly killing them both—but fate had other plans.

She looked at Marvin with pleading eyes. "My

baby."

The horn blared. Someone screamed.

She didn't feel a thing.

## Chapter Twenty-Six

Jenny was crying. "I didn't feel anything, but no one knew. They never knew that I'd already left my body. It was as though I were watching the entire thing unfold from outside of myself."

Meara took a deep breath. She'd heard a lot of life stories in her years as a Regression Therapist, but this story—Erin's story—was up there with the sadder, more tragic ones. Poor Jenny. Both Adala's tragic death and now Erin's, it was no wonder that she was so stalled in this lifetime. The soul can only handle so much at any given time.

"And the baby?"

Jenny furrowed her brow. "Medical help came fairly quickly. Somehow, miraculously, the baby survived.

It was a girl." Jenny's voice caught in her throat. "He named her Emma Erin. E.E. Goebel. And Patrick, he took care of her and raised her on his own. He never fell in love again. Never married again. He said if it wasn't serendipity, then he wanted no part." Jenny paused, her brow still furrowed as if she were contemplating. "He never blamed fate. Because of what happened. He never thought fate was cruel or unjust. He just completely, unconditionally accepted the circumstance."

"Perhaps Patrick's soul was a bit more evolved than Erin's?" Meara suggest gently.

Jenny sniffled and nodded. Meara handed her a tissue and Jenny, still regressed, accepted it gratefully. "Yes, that's it. My Higher Self tells me that is why Patrick was able to raise their daughter on his own and be a good father. Because he knew, deep down, that life was about acceptance. Accepting your mistakes, accepting the cards that are handed to you, accepting the circumstances, but no matter what always trying to make the best of them and know that everything is working out for your highest good." Jenny smiled. "Patrick and Emma were extremely close. Two peas in a pod. And they remembered Erin fondly. They always got both families together—the Goebel's and the Murphy's—in order to celebrate her birthday."

"May I ask your Higher Self how Erin's passing affected the rest of her family and those around her? At one point Jenny had asked about the so-called Butterfly Effect."

"Certainly. I will put it in the most simple of terms. Not everyone's soul that was involved was as spiritually evolved as Patrick's and even Emma's. Erin's father kept his job, but took up a drinking habit that upset the family balance. Mrs. Murphy, not having any solace turned to another man and had an affair which kept on until her own passing some years later and which seemed to only fuel Mr. Murphy's alcoholism. Raffe did not follow either his mother or his father's behaviors, but he did become angrier for some time until he fell in love and had a family of his own. Later, he and Patrick became very close, almost like brothers, along with Henry. Fiona was a poet and a writer. She published numerous works on the fleetingness of life and death, often reflecting on her sister's passing but not delving into despair. Erin's fellow librarians created a memorial in her honor and eventually an entire wing of the library was named after her. The rest of the Goebel's mourned quietly, but were delighted with the addition of their granddaughter, who they considered to be a living example of a miracle. And she was."

"Tell me about Marvin and the driver of the other taxicab." Meara was trying to keep up, scribbling in her notebook.

"Marvin is interesting," the Higher Self said. "Marvin carried a lot of guilt for the remainder of his life, but because he instinctively did all the right things Erin's baby was spared. He kept in contact with Emma until she went off to college, sending her a card on each birthday. Which also happened to be the anniversary of her mother's death. He was a good man. He just could not forgive himself at the soul level. Because we travel in soul circles, Evert was present as Patrick, the one true romantic soulmate of our soul. However, in this life, Mrs. Murphy was not the same mother figure who appeared in the other two incarnations. In this life Jenny's current mother was incarnated as Marvin. The driver of the other taxicab, was not so fortunate in dealing with his guilt. He eventually took his own life, unable to deal with the consequences of his unintended actions. As Keren and Pleagia were incarnations of Hadley, there was no incarnation of Hadley in this particular life. However, Krischen and Nikomedes were incarnations of the taxicab driver. In Jenny's current incarnation, this person is her ex-boyfriend, Kevin."

Meara asked, "What is Jenny's soul to learn from Erin's life"?

"We have learned about unconditional acceptance and that regardless of how things appear, things are always working out for our highest good if we could only accept the circumstances we are given. Furthermore, part of acceptance is forgiveness. Forgiveness not so much for the person who has wronged us—at least as we perceive it—but forgiveness for ourselves. We are so hard on ourselves while on the Earthly plane. If you could see it from our perspective you would see how the guilt each one of you carries weighs like a heavy burden across your shoulders, like a crown of thorns around your heart. If you could learn the peaceful act of acceptance, and in that simple choice to accept the conditions as they have come, then and only then will each of you find the ability to forgive." Jenny's voice sounded serene and joyful.

Meara had to admit it all made sense. She learned just as much from these sessions as did her clients. That's one of the reasons she was so grateful that she had accepted her talents and created a career that allowed her to help others in such profound ways. The Higher Self continued, "If Jenny could see how her mother lives this life in retribution for her perceived guilt in her past incarnation, and could only know the darkness that overtook the soul she knows as Kevin, perhaps then she could learn to accept either of them as they appear to be. People are who they are. If Jenny could learn to accept this fact and forgive both of them for their past, present, and future transgressions, then our soul too will find much peace. Acceptance and forgiveness are the keys."

# Chapter Twenty-Seven

If Jenny had felt drained after experiencing Adala and Menodora's lives, she felt even more exhausted after experiencing the life of Erin. She moved around her apartment with the shades drawn and in her pajamas for three days. Caddie laid curled up on the couch, body still, ears alert and large, brown eyes watching as Jenny moved around the dimly lit room.

After the session, once Meara had brought her back to the current world—if you could think of it as such, Jenny's perception of time and reality seemed to be altering—the first thing she'd noticed was the tissue in her hand. The second thing she'd noticed was the throbbing headache that accompanied crying. Erin's memories were foggy, and Meara had reassured her it was a self-preservation technique because Erin's life strongly overlapped with Jenny's. But all Meara would say is that several of the people Jenny had complex relationships with in her current incarnation were also present in Erin's. She was quick, however, to assure Jenny that once she listened to the recording—which sat unopened in Jenny's e-mail inbox—and read the transcript, the fogginess would disappear and the memories would be crisp and clear. Meara emphasized that Erin also experienced a tragic demise, but that it may be harder than either Adala's or Menodora's for Jenny to process.

*What could be more tragic than dying during the Holocaust and more tragic than the sinking of Atlantis?* Jenny had asked. Meara had only shook her head and assured her that she'd understand once she listened to the session. She also gave Jenny very strict follow-up instructions, scribbled in Meara's flowing cursive:

*-Listen to the session*

*-Cleanse in a salt bath afterward*

*-Try to sit in stillness, breathing deeply, for at least twenty minutes*

*-Sleep on clean sheets*

*-Thank your Higher Self for its guidance*

Jenny stared at the note written on stationary with Meara's monogram in the corner: *MAS*. She bet her middle name was Anne. Meara was Jewish, at least Jenny was pretty sure she was. What if she was a German Jew and her middle name was Adala? That would be weird. Like fate or something. The hair on the back of Jenny's neck prickled. A faint memory. *Patrick.* Jenny shook her head. She couldn't remember, wasn't yet ready to remember. Instead she decided to call Hadley.

"What's going on, JMac?" Hadley answered after the second ring. Even though Jenny's last name was not pronounced like Macdonald, Hadley had started calling her JMac back when Jennifer Lopez became JLo. Just like when Jennifer Lopez had been known as Jenny from the block, guess what nickname Hadley had given her? Too bad the only thing she shared with Jennifer Lopez was the same first name. She wouldn't mind having *her* butt insured for millions of dollars.

Jenny could hear a deeper, bass tone in the background. Jedd. For a second Jenny thought about saying never mind, but she knew Hadley. And she knew that if she did that Hadley would call her right back and if she didn't answer Hadley would show up on her doorstep. She'd made that mistake once before.

"I had my third session with Meara a few days ago."

"Ah, that explains why I haven't heard from you. Hey, hold on." She heard Hadley turn away from the phone and say, "It's important. It's Jenny! Yeah. Okay, see you later!"

"What time is it?"

"That bad? It's like 10 AM Friday. Jedd just left for work." Jedd was his own boss. He was an accountant. Which was weird because Hadley wasn't known to date many accountants, but she and Jedd had some sort of yin-yang thing going on for sure. They both had amazing work ethics and both believed their work was important to improving people's lives—Hadley improved minds and bodies, Jedd improved bank accounts and financial security. Although on the surface the pair seemed unlikely, once you saw them together you realized right away that it all made complete and total sense. Jenny felt a pang. She longed for that feeling.

Jenny rubbed her eyes. "I don't remember much from the session. I've been kind of in a haze, I think."

Hadley said, "That happens. Especially after a really intense session. You need to get out. Return to the land of the living. Come to yoga."

Jenny ignored the request. Or the demand. Depending on how you looked at it. "This time Meara gave me a note. It's, like, instructions for after listening to the session."

The other line was silent a beat then Hadley said, "That means your sessions are over."

"Huh?" Jenny was confused. Didn't she decide when her sessions were over?

"It means your sessions have come full-circle. Your Higher Self has shown you the lives that have led you to your current incarnation as none other than Jenny McClain. Let me guess, the note said to take a salt bath and sit in silence after listening to the recording."

"Yep, did you get the same one?"

"I think everyone does. The salt is to clear out the negativity of the sessions, like any residual stuff that could be hanging around."

"You sound like one of those ghost-hunting shows."

Hadley ignored the comment. "The silence is to meditate, listen for any more instructions from your Higher Self. Light some candles, put on some soft music. You can chant, if it makes you feel more focused."

"I don't chant. I don't meditate."

"It's good advice. It wouldn't kill you to try it once."

"What's with the clean sheets?"

"It's like a fresh start. Trust me it works. The next morning you will feel like a new person—well, like yourself, but better. It'll be like Jenny 2.0"

"I like Jenny 1.0."

"No, you don't. Jenny 1.0 is needy and stagnant. You need Jenny 2.0 who is vibrant, funny, and loveable."

"How do you know?"

"Because Jenny 2.0 is closer to who you truly are."

"Will I ever see Meara again?"

"Probably. She'll probably wait awhile then contact you to meet for coffee or lunch. She came to one of my yoga sessions. She still does sometimes. Just to check in. She knows about Jedd and she seemed really happy with my progress."

"Me too. I'm happy for you. I'm glad you met Jedd."

"What about Greg?"

Jenny had completely forgotten about Greg, having been totally wrapped up in her last session with Meara. Mental head slap. She peered at her phone. No voicemails. "I haven't heard from him yet."

"Don't worry. The Universe doesn't deliver the goods until you're ready." There was a pause. "When are you going to listen to the session?"

"Tonight." Jenny answered automatically. Caddie put down one ear, keeping the other one up like a satellite. Eavesdropper.

"You sure about yoga?"

"Maybe I'll come."

Hadley knew that was a no. "Well, text me later."

"K. And Had?"

"Yeah, JMac?"

"Thanks."

"No problem. Trust me, we've been through worse." Jenny smiled. She knew Hadley was referring to their previous incarnations where their friendship endured. All through time and space. Kind of crazy. And yet it kind of made a whole lot of sense. Hadley hung up and Jenny tossed her phone onto the cushioned coffee table. The last thing she needed to do was obsess over Greg calling her. It had almost been a week. That was way past the three-day rule. Jenny almost laughed out loud. How old was she? Sixteen?

She stood up and stretched then pulled open the

blinds. The day was sunny and the sky was a bright cerulean. The world was coming alive with spring. But it was only April. You never knew in Cleveland. One day it could be seventy degrees in April, the next day you could get half a foot of snow. Jenny felt the strange prickling sensation on the back of her neck again. It was a common thing to say around the area. But at the same time, she felt like she'd heard that before somewhere else. Somewhere that was here, and yet not here. *1921.*

Choosing to ignore the fragment of memory, Jenny turned to Caddie who was still watching her from the couch. The look on the dog's face was disapproving, if a dog could look disapproving.

"Don't look at me like that, Caddie Addie Saddie." She glanced back out the window. People weren't wearing coats, they were wearing light jackets and hooded sweatshirts. This was Jenny's favorite kind of weather. She had told Hadley the truth, she was going to listen to her session tonight—she knew she had to. She had to know what happened and what messages her Higher Self had delivered. These pieces of fractured recollection were going to make her crazy, if wandering around the house in her pajamas and in the dark didn't already classify her as such. The session was going to be emotional, based on hers and Meara's reactions, and afterward she was going to follow Meara's instructions precisely. Yes, she would even do the meditation thing. No one said she had to do it right, if there was even a right way to do such a thing.

Across from the apartment was a large green space of grass, trees, and park benches. Some college-aged guys were playing soccer. *Return to the land of the living.* She'd shower and then take Caddie for a walk. Then she'd bring some coffee to Hadley at the yoga studio. She herself wouldn't downward dog, but she could at least make an appearance. Who knew? Hadley probably had some incense and meditation books and CDs Jenny could borrow. Then maybe she'd swing by the art supply store followed by the drugstore for those bath salts. If she was going to do this, she was going to do it right. Tomorrow she would be Jenny 2.0. She may as well enjoy her last day as Jenny 1.0

∞

Jenny anticipated the evening with a mixture of dread and excitement. She dreaded going in knowing she would relive whatever trauma Erin had experienced; that it would come back into her memory like an old movie reel, a combination of both continuous scenes and fast-forwarded portions. Play. Pause. Play. But she was excited to learn the lessons her Higher Self had to offer and the connections Erin's life offered to Jenny's own. She'd decided to go in with the best attitude possible. Recalling Erin's Irish roots, in addition to the salt she'd purchased and meditation CDs she'd borrowed from Hadley, Jenny had also stopped into one of the locally-owned candle shops and picked up a soy, 'Irish moss' scented candle in a pretty emerald green jar. She didn't know exactly what Irish moss was, but it smelled soft, yet earthy at the same time.

She set her bags on the counter and dropped some food into Caddie's bowl. Then she unpacked the bags, putting the bath salts on the edge of the shower-tub combo. Meara hadn't stipulated a scent, so Jenny had chosen a relaxing lavender. She tossed the meditation CDs onto her bed, where an old boom box was gathering dust in the corner. She supposed she could have just Googled some type of meditation music, but she didn't trust just any randomly generated result. She didn't want to mess this up—if this indeed was the end of the line in her regression experience. Hadley had handed her two CDs that she said were her favorite—one consisted of tracks with what Hadley had called *mantras,* Sanskrit words that helped keep your mind focused. The other CD was strictly instrumental. Jenny figured she'd go with whatever intuitively felt right, if anything that's one of the major lessons she'd learned from her time with Meara. Trust your intuition. Adala had done it. Menodora almost hadn't.

Jenny made her way back to the kitchen. Caddie's bowl was emptied and she was already curled up, staking her claim on one end of the couch. Jenny grabbed the candle off the counter, lit it, and placed it on a shelf above the couch, next to photographs of Caddie, her family on vacation in Ocean City, and one of her and Hadley at the grand opening of her yoga studio. Next, she grabbed the soft, faux fur blanket off the armchair and dragged it over to the couch, draping it over both herself and Caddie. She turned her phone to silent and tossed it onto the coffee table, before grabbing her MacBook. The screen lit up her face, in an eerie, blue-green glow. She'd kept the lights dim on purpose; the sun was already set and the evening was fast fading into night. With nimbly navigating fingers, Jenny pulled open her e-mail inbox and clicked on the message from Meara that was marked almost a week ago. She opened both the transcript and the audio recording. It was time to reacquaint herself with the life of Erin Murphy.

## Chapter Twenty-Eight

The next morning Jenny laid in bed staring at the ceiling. It was early. Early enough that the room was still cast in shades of gray. The sun was only just rising. Caddie was curled in a ball, beneath the comforter, near the foot of the bed. Jenny was grateful for the warm body curled near her calves. She shivered. Erin's life had invaded Jenny's consciousness so vividly, so tangibly, that she'd truly felt as though she were Erin. Maybe, since Erin's soul and Jenny's soul were one and the same, it was her reliving a deep-seated memory of her own. Not one of Jenny's, but one of her own essence. She closed her eyes against the darkness. That was too deep.

What really had Jenny reeling was the revelation about Marvin and the driver of the other taxicab. If Kevin was the driver of that car, then how come he wasn't begging for her forgiveness? How come he had treated her so poorly and disappointed her over and over again, then broke up with her in the lamest of ways? She answered her own questions before she could even process them: Because *her* life lessons were about forgiveness and acceptance, beauty and cruelty, and unconditional love. She opened her eyes to the familiar shadows of the room. Only Kevin and Kevin's Higher Self knew what his life lessons were supposed to be. Despite the paths that our Higher Self arranged for us, Jenny knew that there was still free-will, thus the taxicab driver's early demise. *Accept and forgive.*

Then there was Marvin. Sweet, Marvin, who had tried to get in between the careening car and his pregnant patron. Jenny closed her eyes again, feeling the sting behind her eyelids and the burning itch in her nose that meant she was about to cry. Marvin, when incarnated as Sophia did not have the best interests of Menodora at heart, but now had tried to make up for it with the ultimate of sacrifices, only to fail—at least apparently fail. He lived the rest of his life with a heart full of guilt like a lead weight in his chest. Jenny groaned. Somehow it all made so much sense. Why her mother was so overbearing, always trying to set her up and marry her off. It was to make up for something she wasn't even aware had ever even happened. *Accept and forgive.*

And sweet Patrick. Jenny immediately recognized those eyes too. The deep familiarity that transported her back to Adala and Evert. It wasn't even the fact that both men had blue eyes and blonde hair, it was something else. The warm knowingness. There was another wisp of memory, a cobweb somewhere in the back of her brain. She'd had that feeling another time. But when? There was no incarnation of Evert or Patrick in her Atlantean life. Just Nikomedes. Kevin. She shook her head. The image was deep below the surface and the water was stagnant.

She opened her eyes again and this time the room was slowly filling with the white light of early morning. Taking her pajama sleeve, she wiped the tears from her eyes. Even though she'd done the salt bath and the meditation, and even though she'd thanked her Higher Self for the messages of her past lives, her heart still felt heavy. The small "*o*" of surprise on Erin's face as Jenny felt herself being pulled out of the body, hovering and watching from the safety of above, as the taxicab caromed into her body. Jenny—as Erin, but did it matter if they were truly one and the same?—felt warm arms wrap around her now levitating body. She was overcome with the deepest sense of love, pure, unadulterated, unconditional love. A love so sure, and so steadfast that no matter what she did, she could do no wrong, and was seen as a perfect, pure essence of the very love that was now filling her every cell. Erin was right. She hadn't felt a thing.

Jenny swung her legs over the edge of the bed and sat up a bit too fast, closing her eyes to the dizziness that ensued. Caddie growled at the disruption. She was the anti-dog: Caddie slept in later than most humans. Jenny opened her eyes and snatched up the glass of water from her nightstand and took a tentative sip, waiting for her equilibrium to be restored. Why hadn't Meara's instructions worked? A flash of a framed wedding photograph, a beautiful 1920s, flapper style wedding. Dark hair and large stone-colored eyes that should have been staring at the photographer were instead returning the deep gaze of the tall, blonde man who was also ignoring the photographer and staring into the eyes of his bride. Jenny knew then why the instructions hadn't worked and she also knew what she had to do. She stood up, slipping her feet into her favorite, worn slippers.

Quietly, as to not further disturb the Queen of All Dogs, she shuffled out of the room and down the hallway to her art studio.

∞

Whenever Jenny was in the studio, she worked with a sense of timelessness. It didn't speed up or slow down, she just lost all sense of it. The other canvas paintings were leaned against the window sill. This room had four, tall narrow windows in a row with a ledge—too narrow to be a bench seat, but the perfect place to prop up paintings. The canvases weren't large, twenty inches by twenty inches, short enough so the windows let in unfiltered golden light. Dust particles danced in its beam. She stepped back taking in the latest addition to what had quickly become a collection. Adala, Menodora, now Erin.

Adala's eyes had radiated strength and courage, painted with bold golden browns, they hinted at the love she knew and of the atrocities she experienced. Adala knew that love sometimes required great sacrifice. Menodora's eyes, like the cerulean sea of Atlantis itself, reflected back her beauty and a sort of naivety. A sisterly bond that had spanned multiple lifetimes, Menodora knew that with Pleagia by her side she could do anything, and yet there was an innocence about her that made her seem almost like a mythological nymph. And then there were Erin's eyes.

Jenny stepped so far back that she was now almost standing in the doorway. Round, slate-colored eyes looked back at her, fringed with long, curled, black lashes. A dark brown eyebrow arched in such a way as to suggest that Erin knew something Jenny didn't. And maybe she did. Just because Jenny had experienced an accelerated account of Erin's life didn't mean she knew everything, at least not on the surface. She acknowledged that at a deeper level, there was some knowing, but a life still deserved its own secrets, its own hidden gems for the person living it and the person living it only. Jenny felt it helped retain some of the integrity—the meaningfulness—of that life.

The eyes seemed fathomless, and yet there was a softness about them. There was also a resoluteness. Erin was so sure of herself, Jenny realized as she cocked her head to meet the gaze that looked back at her. Sure of herself in life and even in her death. She had only been ten when she came to America and she'd lived the American Dream, attending school, getting a job, falling in love...having a child. Jenny let out a wistful sigh. It seemed contradictory. She knew each of these incarnations were a part of her…a part of her…essence, and yet she felt inexplicably connected to Erin Murphy-Goebel. Maybe it was the simple fact that they were both Irish, or maybe it was that Jenny deeply-longed for the things that Erin had built for herself: independence, unconditional love, family, selflessness and forgiveness. Erin's first thoughts at her death were not at the loss of her life, of being able to ever hold her baby girl, but of the pain her death would cause others: *they didn't know she hadn't felt a thing.* The so-called butterfly effect. Jenny let out a shiver.

As she looked at the three pairs of eyes, Jenny realized she'd experienced the majority of each life while in her late teens and early twenties. That was around how old she had been when she met Kevin-who-was-Nikomedes-who-was-the-taxicab-driver. They'd been together for three years. Now a year had passed since their break-up and she'd be turning thirty in only a couple of more weeks. It seemed the other women had accomplished so much in such a short period before their untimely deaths. And yet, here she was. A realization came over her—something she'd later chalk up to the lingering effects of communicating with her Higher Self—that perhaps she'd been given the additional time that the other women hadn't. Meara had said during one of the sessions that her soul was old and wise. Maybe she'd just gone too far astray. Another sigh, but this one less pensive and more filled with relief, as if letting go.

She had to admit, it had worked. The act of painting, of paying tribute to the brief life that had been Erin's, had made her feel better. She felt as though her heart had lightened just a bit. A crescendo of Mozart's *Requiem* erupted from the bedroom. Jenny darted across the hall, where Caddie was still tightly curled, only lifting her head to shoot Jenny a withering glare at being disturbed.

"Whatever," Jenny mumbled reaching across the bed to the makeshift, ceramic garden stool night stand, where her phone was still plugged in from the night before. She assumed it would be Hadley or her mom. She disconnected the phone from the charger and put it up to her ear without glancing at the caller ID.

"Hey," she said by way of greeting.

"Hey," came the response, only the voice didn't belong to either Hadley or her mother. Jenny felt her heart catch in her throat and her stomach complete a somersault. The voice was deep, a baritone. And it definitely belonged to a male. Even the simple *hey* made her palms break into a clammy sweat. The voice continued, "This is Greg."

"Oh, yeah. Hi. Sorry about that, I thought it was my mom or my best friend." She knew she was rambling. It was one part nerves and one part surprise that he'd called.

"Sorry, I didn't give you a call sooner. I was out of town at a conference." *Ohhh, that's why he hadn't called!* He wasn't even home! Jenny felt her heart surge with relief. That response was way better than him not being interested, yet somehow she had known that wasn't true.

"Oh, no big deal. I bet that was a good time." The only reason she said it is because she didn't know the appropriate response. *Oh, I'd just assumed you were uninterested like every other guy in the history of the world.*

Greg actually laughed. "Yeah, a room full of ophthalmologists isn't exactly a good time. Too much fun and someone could poke an eye out!" He paused. Jenny's breath caught in her throat. And then she realized he'd made a joke. She let out a nervous giggle, hoping he wouldn't notice the awkward pause from her nervousness.

"Good one. It couldn't have been all that bad."

"No, you're right, it wasn't. I learned a lot.

Actually, now that I'm back in town, I'd love to meet you for a picnic in the park if you're free anytime soon, and maybe I could, uh, tell you about it?" Jenny's nerves softened; he was nervous too. She had a flash—a recollection of memory not of her own accord—of a picnic in a park, laying beneath a tree, but it faded as quickly as it came.

"Um, yeah that would be great. When did you have in mind?"

"Well, I was thinking today…if that's okay…if you're not already busy…"

Jenny's heart leaped. "No, not busy. I'm free." *Ugh, how lame. Nope totally free, just sitting around listening to past-life regressions and painting pictures with my dog.* Mental head-slap.

"Really?" The eagerness in his voice was undisguised. "Great! How about around one? The park with the boat rentals? We can meet at the boathouse."

"Sounds good. See you at one," Jenny's words tumbled out in a breath of excitement.

"See you at one," Greg's voice echoed the same underlying sense of anticipation.

The call ended. Jenny stared at the Home Screen. Then flipped over from her stomach to her back, a smile spread wide across her face. She stared at the ceiling, her heart still pounding enthusiastically. She clutched her phone to her chest as if it were some sort of sacred talisman. A guy had finally asked her out, a guy her own mother had picked out no less, and the real kicker was he seemed just as eager to see her again as she was to see him.

*Well,* she thought, *this was something new.* Maybe new wasn't so bad. Maybe new was really, really good. She rolled her eyes at her own sappiness, but it didn't diminish the truth of the words.

Jenny 2.0.

# Chapter Twenty-Nine

Before Jenny met Greg at the boat rental, she needed to make a couple stops. She pulled into the driveway of the familiar, pale yellow Cape Cod. Normally, perhaps you'd expect a house painted yellow to have white shutters, but not the McClain's. Jenny's mother had insisted on having green shutters—which over the years had become a faded lime. The shutters matched little green planter boxes, which her mother had yet to fill with annuals this spring. beneath the windows to the formal dining room and her father's office. The familiar white rocking chairs greeted her from the front porch.

This was the house she'd grown up in. The driveway curb gave a rough bump as Jenny pulled in. It wasn't often that she drove further east into the more suburby-suburbs and made surprise house calls. She slammed the door to her silver, Chrysler Sebring. She'd picked the silver on purpose because it hid the dirt best, and she wouldn't have to wash it as often as, say, a black or red car. Usually, Jenny's father opened the door when he heard her pull in. Today was no different.

"Well, this is an unexpected surprise," he said by way of greeting. He gave her a quick squeeze. "You look nice."

"Thanks. I can't stay long though. Just stopping by. Is Mom around? Has she left for Zumba yet?" Jenny slipped her black, Converse sneakers off and left them by the door, one of her mother's pet peeves was wearing shoes in the house. The effect Jenny had gone for was relaxed-chic, her favorite sneakers, some knit skinny jeans, a tank top, and a wide-necked sweatshirt that had *Nama'stay in bed* screen-printed across the front in a white cursive, a joke from Hadley instead of the traditional Sanskrit: Namaste. She'd pulled her brown hair into a neat ponytail, threw on foundation, mascara, and lip gloss and called it a day. This was slightly less effort than she'd put in for a more traditional date—say for dinner or drinks, but this was a picnic, and dressing in some of her favorite pieces helped her to feel more comfortable and just a little less nervous.

Her mother was standing in the kitchen drinking a green juice. She was wearing a bright pink V-neck shirt that had *Zumba!* scrolled across the front and strange, black drawstring bottomed sweatpants, that were also probably ordered from the Zumba catalogue because no other person in her right mind would go out in public wearing them, unless they were a hip-hop dancer, which her mother was certainly not. Her sneakers matched her shirt and she had a matching headband to keep her blonde, springy curls away from her face during class. Besides the ridiculous outfit, for a second, if you didn't know that she was fifty-seven-years-old, you'd think she was about forty. Her brown eyes widened when Jenny appeared.

"Is everything okay?" she asked.

"Is it that weird that I stopped by?"

"Mary Anne will be here in ten minutes to pick me up for Zumba." Jenny heard her father go back to his office and begin typing on his old, typewriter. Her father sometimes wrote articles about local going-ons for their county newspaper. He insisted on using the typewriter and sending them by snail mail. Even though it probably created more work for them, the newspaper somehow still hired him.

"I won't take more than ten minutes."

"Oh." Her mother's eyes narrowed. "Are you wearing makeup? You never wear makeup." Which was true, unless she had an art exhibition, job interview, or date, she went bare-faced, freckles and all.

Jenny shifted uncomfortably in her stocking feet. "Um, yeah. I have a thing."

"A thing?" Her mother chugged the rest of her green juice before sticking it upside down in the dishwasher.

"A date." It came out barely audible. But her mother whirled around, a different look in her eyes, an excited sparkle that had been absent much of the time lately.

"Is it Greg?" Her mother breathed and for a second it was as if two girlfriends were having a gossip session. It was a new feeling.

Jenny nodded. "He called me and we're meeting at the park. The one with the boat rentals. He wanted to have a picnic."

Usually this was the part where her mother would tell her not to mess it up, but instead, her hand fluttered to cover her heart. "That is just so sweet! He is such a good son to Edna, but she can't stand to have him under foot all the time! She does love her independence. Edna's a wild one." She chuckled. "I thought he might be interested in you."

"You did?"

"Well, of course. You're beautiful and smart." Jenny wished her mother could add *successful* to that list of adjectives. "And you're a good person."

"I am?"

Her mother's brow furrowed "Of course you are, Honey." There was a honk from outside. Mary Anne. "Oops, looks like Mary Anne's a bit early. Ted must have been driving her nuts. If anything she's usually late." She leaned over and picked up a small, floral-printed tote bag, then turned to Jenny with a soft smile. "I'm happy for you, Sweetheart."

"Wait. Mom." Jenny instinctively put out a hand and placed it on her mother's shoulder. Their family wasn't very touchy-feely, or happy-huggy like those families Jenny had watched as a kid on Disney and Nickelodeon. "I wanted to stop by to thank you. Thank you for introducing me to Greg. For some reason I can't explain, I have a good feeling about it."

Her mother smiled, a genuine full-toothed smile, not the usual smirks and disapproving grimaces Jenny was used to receiving. "I have a good feeling about it, too."

The next words rushed out before Jenny could stop them. "I know I don't always show it, but I know that when you do stuff like you did with Greg showing up at dinner, that you're just doing it because you love me and want to see me happy."

The smile faded, replaced with a look of concern. She lowered the tote bag to the counter. "Well, of course that's what I want for you. Any decent mother wants her child to feel loved and find happiness."

Sophia's face, followed by Marvin's flashed through Jenny's mind like a game of *Guess Who.* Sophia had thought she was making Menodora happy, giving her a better life by marrying her off to a wealthy upper classman. And then there was Marvin, a mere acquaintance, willing to step in front of a careening taxi in order to save Erin's life. These, too, were her mother. Only her mother had no idea. She had no idea how selfless and loving she was. Jenny had had no idea until now.

She found herself throwing her arms around her mother's broad shoulders. "Thank you. Thank you for loving me and accepting me as I am. I always thought you were trying to change me, but you were just trying to help me to be happy. I'm sorry that I always took your efforts the wrong way."

Her mother hugged her back with unsure arms. "I forgive you even though I'm not quite sure what I am forgiving you for. What's this all about, Jenny?" She pulled away and looked at her daughter.

But Jenny was smiling, because now she understood. "I forgive you too, Mom."

Mrs. McClain looked confused. Mary Anne beeped again, this time a double-tap. She glanced down the hallway then back at Jenny. Something had shifted in her eyes, something that normally Jenny may not have noticed, but now that she understood, she couldn't help but notice. A glint in her mother's eye that was a mix of relief and understanding. One soul identifying another, despite the lifetimes that each wore like disguises throughout time and space. Her mother may not understand the change on the surface, but deep down she would recognize the shift in the relationship between her and her daughter, the shift that could only come when two souls acknowledged the lesson that had been learned. "I better go." She picked up her tote bag and gave Jenny a real hug, her face dissolved back into a smile. "You have fun on your date with Greg."

"Thanks." By the time Jenny got out the words her mother was already down the hallway and heading out the front door.

∞

The second stop she needed to make was Hadley's studio. On the way Jenny swung through the drive-thru at the Starbucks. The little chime Hadley had hung over the door went off as Jenny entered, drink carrier in hand. The front of the studio—where the shop was located—was void of Hadley, but filled with all sorts of crystals, books, incense, essential oils, and artisan soaps and body products from local merchants. Sometimes Hadley had a nice, high-school aged girl named Star (no, joke) who would man the shop and take in new clients. As of right now, Hadley was the main instructor, but her business was quickly growing and soon she'd have to hire even more additional instructors in order to keep the small class sizes that made her studio so desirable.

After about a minute Hadley entered from the studio to the right of the shop. It was in between classes. Jenny had the schedule memorized. Hadley grinned when she realized who it was, or saw that there was coffee, Jenny couldn't be sure which.

She accepted the soy chai latte and nodded. "Thanks. Nice shirt." Hadley herself was wearing black leggings with mesh panels up the sides and a plum-colored racer back tank that said *Coffee.Yoga. Om.* She still looked serene, so hot yoga must be the next class. There were too many yoga variants of which to keep track, so Jenny was just happy she could remember the schedule. Hadley squinted and leaned forward. "Are you wearing makeup?"

"You sound like my mother," Jenny chided.

"He called." It wasn't a question. It was a statement.

"He did."

"The cleansing worked, then?"

"I don't know about that exactly. Maybe it's just a coincidence that he called after my last session with Meara."

Hadley climbed onto the stool behind the shop counter. She shook her head. "No coincidences. Synchronicities, fate, destiny, serendipity—yes, but never coincidences. There's no such thing."

Jenny had a flash of a blonde-haired, blue-eyed

face, but it was blurry. *Serendipity.*

"You realize some people would point out that all those other new-agey, *woo-woo* words you used would be classified as no such thing. Not the other way around."

Hadley shrugged. "That's their problem." She took a sip of chai. And Jenny did the same, opting for just a plain, skim latte, not wanting to spoil her appetite before her date. "So what time are you meeting him?"

Jenny looked at the small, digital clock on the counter. "Twenty minutes?"

"Like twenty minutes from now?" Jenny nodded. "Oh, a man who goes after what he wants. I admire that."

"We're going on a picnic in the park."

Hadley raised an eyebrow. "That sounds lovely. It also sounds very un-Jenny-like."

"It was his idea. I thought it sounded fun."

"Do I know you?"

"Jenny 2.0. It's good to try new things."

"Meara is a miracle worker."

"No, she's not. She's a regression therapist." Jenny didn't want to be late, so she started to head toward the door. The next yoga class started in twenty minutes too and students would be arriving soon. "Now, if she could get me to start doing yoga and meditating regularly, then maybe I'd consider her a miracle worker."

"Stranger things have happened," Hadley smiled.

Jenny smiled back. "Yeah, they have."

## Chapter Thirty

It was warm for spring in Cleveland, where it was known to snow well into April some years. Jenny pulled the Sebring into the gravel parking lot, driving slowly to avoid causing too many dings and bangs. The parking lot was practically full. Happy, formerly snowed-in people emerged from their houses like flower buds after the winter thaw. She found a spot way in the back, almost near the entrance, but didn't care. The four months of summer always went by too fast and Jenny was determined to enjoy them, not let them go by unnoticed. Jenny 1.0 would have just blown right past like a bull in a china shop.

Something had changed. Jenny could feel it as she hopped the wooden fence and crossed the grass to the asphalt bicycle path, heading toward the boat rental station. Hadley was right. She *was* different. At first Jenny couldn't pinpoint it. Then, after thinking about it as she got ready for her date with Greg, and taking Caddie for a quick walk around the apartment complex, she'd realized what it was. Her sense of time had changed. She no longer had the feeling of urgency that used to always seem to hang over her head. *Graduate. Get a job. Get married. Have babies. Retire. Hurry, hurry, hurry.* As she'd applied mascara she'd noticed she hadn't even glanced at the clock since waking that morning. So she did. Only a few hours had passed. She had plenty of time to get ready, swing by her parents' house, and stop to see Hadley. There was no hurry. Because what was the point? When you learn—and experience proof—that life is indefinite, the sense of urgency is simply no longer there. Jenny wondered if that was the secret to Hadley's always relaxed demeanor.

Now, as she walked the quarter mile to the boat house, Jenny took in the kids playing kickball in the green space to her left, and the sun sparkling across the gray-green water of Lake Erie to her right. Large Oak, Buckeye, and Maple trees—some already in full bloom—draped periodic patches of shade across her path. Kids and adults alike whizzed by on bicycles. There was a brief flash of a memory, a blonde-haired man ahead of her on a red bicycle. She could feel the rough seat beneath her and her feet pedaling on a bicycle of her own as she watched the man ahead of her turn and give her a flirtatious grin. And just like that the memory was gone.

Jenny blinked to reorient herself and continued her walk. She was almost there; she could see the cluster of customers looking to rent a boat for the afternoon and enjoy some time on the lake. The glimpses of memories weren't bothersome. She considered them a sort of residual effect of the regressions, only this time they seemed to have lingered a bit longer than usual. They were more vibrant too, as if she were watching a movie play out on a screen, only in the first person point of view.

As she neared the boat house she recognized Greg's tall form. He was average build, not out of shape, but not exactly a triathlete either. And that was okay. Exercise wasn't exactly super high on Jenny's priority list anyways. His dark hair fluttered in the breeze and he was wearing aviator sunglasses. He had on jeans and what looked like a vintage t-shirt of some kind. As Jenny's mother always liked to tell her: everything old is new again. There was a reusable tote bag from Whole Foods draped over his shoulder and he looked completely at ease standing in the shade of the boat house, waiting. For her. Recognition crossed his features and he put up an arm in greeting. She waved back and felt her heart begin to pound in her ribcage. When she got nearer, she noticed his t-shirt was for some sci-fi British TV show she didn't watch—*Doctor Who* something or other—a show that no other guy she'd ever dated had watched, nor would she probably have ever considered dating a guy who watched geeky, science fiction shows with cryptic titles. Except this time, she didn't seem to care. That's when she noticed his shoes and broke into a grin.

Black Converse sneakers.

∞

Before she could properly greet him, Greg reached into the Whole Foods bag and pulled out a bouquet of floppy-petaled, vibrant flame-colored flowers. He thrust the bouquet in between them, avoiding the awkward, I-don't-really-know-you-acquaintance-hug or worse side hug. Or even worse—a handshake. Jenny accepted the flowers, which had a clear plastic bag banded tightly around the stems.

"They're poppies," Greg explained, but Jenny had already identified the flower.

"Are you trying to sedate me?" she asked. Greg's face went ashen and Jenny quickly added, "I'm kidding! Poppies were the flowers in *The Wizard of Oz,* when Dorothy and the gang are headed to Oz and the Wicked Witch casts the spell. They all fall asleep in a field of poppies." Greg's face regained some color. *Way to almost blow it, McClain,* Jenny chided to herself. Out loud she said, "They're really beautiful. Thanks."

"Oh, you're welcome. I stopped at Whole Foods to grab a few things, then I saw them there all cheerful, with their petals seeming to wave at me. I couldn't resist." He looked down at her. "I like natural beauty." It sounded as if he were still talking about the flowers, but Jenny got the sneaking suspicion he was complimenting her. Before she could think twice about it, he took his free hand and gestured down the bicycle path, away from the boathouse. "Should we find a suitable picnic table and have some lunch?"

"Sounds great." They fell into the flow of bicyclers, rollerbladers, hoverboarders, and speedwalkers clogging up the beginning of the more than ten mile path that ran along the lake, connecting several of the suburbs that lined the shore. The silence stretched between them—Jenny clutching her flowers and Greg clutching his

Whole Foods bag—but it wasn't uncomfortable, more amiable. She recalled how nervous he'd sounded on the phone, and let's be honest first dates pretty much are always awkward, so she was relieved he seemed as nervous as she was. Luckily, the hubbub around them was a welcome distraction.

Jenny watched as a woman with a short, curled bob whizzed by on a retro-looking cruiser bike, a more stream-lined version of the ones that made her think of the 1950s. She felt a momentary surge of recognition, but it quickly vanished as the woman turned to say something to whoever was supposed to be behind her. Her face was young and her skin porcelain, she had on little round sunglasses and red lipstick. Jenny could only dream of being that hipster. It just wasn't her style. Not seeing who she was looking for the woman turned forward and continued down the bicycle path.

"How about over there?" Greg stopped, pulling Jenny aside so she wouldn't get run over on the path. He was barely touching her elbow and yet Jenny could feel a surge of heat, a warmth that spread through her chest and then dipped into her stomach. His fingers dropped as he pointed to the spot he'd identified as a good place to picnic. It was a clustered area of five or six wooden tables. A broken, rusted out grill stood sentry beside each table.

That's when Jenny saw the tree. A lone Buckeye tree, with its yellow flowers and green leaves just beginning to emerge, beckoned them. It was a few yards away from the picnic tables. "How about there? On the grass beneath that tree?"

"I didn't bring a picnic blanket or anything."

"That's okay. We can just sit in the grass." She didn't know why she suggested it. It went against her anti-bug policy to sit in the grass. She just felt compelled to say it. Just as she had felt the same compulsion when she'd slipped her phone number into Greg's palm. "It'll be more authentic that way."

Greg shrugged good-naturedly, "If you say so."

They walked toward the Buckeye tree. It was quieter and away from the rest of the people, who were happy to be outdoors after several months of hibernation. As they walked Jenny could feel the warmth of the sun penetrating through the shoulders of her sweatshirt and warming the top of her head. She could hear children yelling excitedly, a dog barking, and a woman's musical laughter in the distance. Everything seemed more beautiful: the grass seemed greener, the sky bluer; it was as if all her senses were heightened, only she couldn't give a rational explanation why.

Another moment of recognition: her head resting in the lap of a young man as she read a book. Then it was gone. As if the memory was as intangible as the air itself. Jenny instinctively shook her head. Maybe she could knock the memory out. Or knock it back in.

Greg gave her a strange look. "Are you okay?"

"Yeah. Just a bee."

"A bee? Already? I think it's a little early for that."

"Well, you know what they say about global warming and the collapsing bee colonies…and all that." In actuality, Jenny had no idea what was said about the bee colonies because she refused to watch the news. In her opinion, news and mass media was full of scare tactics that didn't seem to serve her and only made her feel depressed. Besides, if the zombie apocalypse started, she was sure she'd hear about it with enough time to break into a convenience store and stock up on water, gossip magazines, and other essentials—like Milky Way bars.

"Actually, I don't know all that they say. I never have time to watch or read anything it feels like. Whenever I sit down, something from work snaps up my attention." He plopped down and sat the Whole Foods bag beside him. Jenny followed suit, but still clutched the flowers as if they could help tether her to the present moment.

"So you're a workaholic, huh?"

Greg scooted back toward the tree trunk and leaned against it. He looked so relaxed. "Not so much the work. More the helping people part. I can be on-call sometimes if an emergency arises."

*I like helping people, Sir.*

"Wait. Don't you just, like, give people prescriptions for contact lenses or whatever?"

"That's an optometrist. I'm an ophthalmologist. I actually diagnose diseases, treat injuries, and perform surgeries." He shrugged. "Conduct research, write journal articles. The usual doctor stuff."

"You're an *actual* doctor? Not just some stuffy, overly educated guy who got his doctorate and says he's a doctor?" She could hardly believe her mother had set her up with an *actual* doctor. She just figured he worked at the glasses store in the mall or something, not in a real medical facility.

"Gregory Patrick Godfrey, MD at your service."

"Your middle name is Patrick?"

"Yeah. German-Irish roots and all that." Jenny recalled her own voice describing to Meara a tall, blonde gentleman who had tried to steal her taxicab. His name had been Patrick. Erin and Patrick. *Coincidence,* Jenny reasoned. *No such thing,* retaliated Hadley's voice in her head. The butterflies in her stomach seemed to agree. "You don't look so great. You just went pale. Are you sure you're okay?" He turned, the sun filtering through the trees' leaves and speckling the top of his head. Out of the Whole Foods bag, he pulled out a plastic container of grapes and offered it to her.

She took it and popped a couple of fat, purple ones into her mouth. "Thanks."

"Better?"

"Much." She watched as he pulled out other things: chunks of cheese and salami, cucumber-infused water, and a bar of raw, dark chocolate. Well, you couldn't say Greg wasn't healthy. Jenny wished her own diet was this well-rounded. She relied heavily on Ramen noodles, Diet Dr. Pepper, and pints of double chocolate chunk ice cream. Luckily, she somehow remained relatively slender, but after watching her mother over the years she knew Zumba would most likely be in her future too. Or whatever the latest workout craze would be twenty years from now.

When he was done pulling out stuff, she narrowed her eyes at him. "You don't look like a doctor."

He smiled taking a chunk of cheese and a piece of salami and popping it into his own mouth. "Tell me. What does a doctor look like then?"

"You know, like, all suit and tie. And stuff." Jenny felt her own cheeks grow hot, maybe a little well-deserved payback for her *Wizard of the Oz* comment earlier about the poppies.

This time Greg laughed and it was hearty and full. "Yeah, that's pretty much the antithesis of what I am."

"You don't wear a suit and tie?"

"Not if I can help it." His face turned serious. "I'd rather be known for my work than for my wardrobe. I can't necessarily say the same for all my colleagues."

Jenny nodded as she helped herself to some of the cheese and salami. "There's some truth in that." Greg brandished two silicone wine glasses out of the Whole Foods bag, filled one with some of the cucumber-water and offered it to her. She thanked him, waiting to take a sip before he filled his own. When he was done she held her glass up in the air. "To new friends."

He clinked his glass against hers, the soft silicone squishing against each other. "To new beginnings."

# Chapter Thirty-One

The date played on an endless, happy loop in Jenny's mind. Sure, it had been a little awkward at times, but it always was when you were first getting to know someone. Greg's laughter played like the soundtrack to the movie. They moved on to discuss her art career, or lack thereof, or as he'd put it—her stalled career. What really caught her off guard was when he'd said nonchalantly that he admired someone who could follow her heart's desire, despite the pressure from family and friends to follow one path over another. Usually, when she said she was a painter or an artist, she got strange, sympathetic looks as if she were tainted, or couldn't hold a "real" job. She could, but she didn't need to yet. If it ever came to that she was more than willing to admit that her art should remain a hobby. Defeat just wasn't ready to be admitted yet.

She'd asked if ophthalmology was his heart's desire and he'd taken the time to answer her thoughtfully, that his mother—Edna—was a bit on the pushy side and had sort of manipulated him into the career path by paying for all of his schooling. And yet, he'd found the silver lining in the fact that he refused to conform to the status quo and that he genuinely enjoyed helping people. The bottom line being that it didn't matter the tools or the means, as long as he was able to improve someone's life.

It was strange talking to someone, besides Hadley of course, who seemed to have the same values and convictions. Sure, they didn't like the same TV shows, as the conversation had later revealed, but Jenny had felt a warmness spread throughout her as they sat beneath the Buckeye tree—a feeling that seemed to extend from the top of her head to the bottom of her feet.

The feelings weren't logical, they'd only met twice, and yet even though they were just getting to know one another, Jenny had the feeling that they'd known each other forever. In fact, she'd reasoned with herself, maybe they had. Gregory Patrick Godfrey. Was it a coincidence that Greg's middle name was the same as Erin's beau?

Hadley would say there's no such thing as coincidences. She'd say it was synchronistic. Fate. Destiny. Then Jenny recalled the word from her regression. The same word that Patrick had used to describe how he and Erin had met in the taxicab on that rainy morning in Cleveland: serendipity. Was it possible? Could her mother's soul somehow have orchestrated this meeting between the husband and wife whose time together had been cut short so drastically, not once but twice? There was only one person she knew of who could help her answer those questions.

∞

Meara suggested meeting at one of Hadley's yoga classes then grabbing brunch right after. Naturally, Jenny said yes. Also, it was not necessarily Jenny's first choice. Despite the love she had for her best friend, she still couldn't comprehend why people would get up early on a weekend to go to a yoga class where the room was eighty degrees and then move through swift succession of yoga poses. What part of that sounded like fun to anyone? No one in their right mind, Jenny reasoned. Perhaps she wasn't of right mind when her curiosity began overriding her logic receptors, because she had practically said yes before Meara could even finish the question.

That's why instead of sleeping in on a Saturday morning, she was pulling on a pair of leopard print leggings and a purple, racerback tank top, when she'd much rather still be lying in bed. Sometimes the need to know trumped the need to sleep in. She begrudgingly swept her hair into a ponytail, and then dug through the hall closet until she found her yoga mat. It was rolled up in the back corner with a fur-lined trapper cap over the top. At least it had other practical uses.

It was a cool morning, so Jenny grabbed a lightweight hoodie and pulled it over head before tucking her yoga mat under her arm and heading to the car port. As she backed out, the questions she had for Meara floated to the surface of her mind, like bubbles needing to be popped. The yoga studio wasn't far away, about a fifteen minute drive. Jenny easily found some street parking almost directly in front of the studio. *Because only crazy people are up this early to sweat,* she reasoned. As she got out of her Sebring, a bright yellow Kia Soul pulled into a spot across the street. Jenny could tell from the driver's profile that it was Meara. It amused her that Meara would have such a sunny, happy-colored car.

Meara got out of the car, tugging a bag with a rolled up yoga mat strapped to it. Her bobbed hair was pushed behind her ears. She looked lithe as she darted across the street toward the yoga studio, in her black leggings and oversized, tunic sweater. When she was almost across the street, she noticed Jenny standing on the sidewalk waiting for her, and waved in greeting.

"Hey! How are you feeling?" she asked, throwing her arms around Jenny in a tight, bone-crushing hug. No handshakes here. This was not the *business* Meara, Jenny realized, this was the older, wiser *friend* Meara.

"Okay. I mean good!"

"Well, which is it?"

"Both?" It was a question and not a statement. Hadley was already in the studio talking to some students about asana. There was ten minutes before class would start. She gave a small wave to Hadley, then followed Meara over to the storage benches in between the studio and the shop. Meara began unstrapping her yoga mat and slipping out of her orthopedic flip-flops.

"Did you follow my directions?" Her voice was soft and calm, but her eyes appeared worried.

"I did."

"But..."

"I don't know. I feel like I still experience flashes of Erin's memories. They're quick and gone almost as soon as they appear." The yoga mat felt sweaty in Jenny's hands and then she remembered this was Hot Yoga and it was going to be almost 100 degrees in the studio. She shrugged her hoodie over her head and crammed it into a cubby with her sneakers.

"That's not so strange," Meara pulled out a yoga mat-sized towel. Why hadn't Jenny thought of that? If she was sweating, she'd be sliding all over the mat and probably break an ankle. Luckily, she was pretty sure if she told Hadley, there were probably extra towels lying around somewhere that she could use. "Sometimes, if a past life was fairly recent or if you felt particularly connected, you could experience some residual effects. They should fade over time."

Some upbeat, instrumental music started, signaling that students could start finding a spot to lay out their mats. Jenny followed Meara into the studio. There were some golden squares of sunlight near the row of windows on the right side of the studio and Meara rolled out her mat directly onto one of the squares. Jenny opted to go beside her, to the left, so that she would be closer to Hadley's instruction. She didn't exactly know what she was doing and she knew her friend would offer body alignment corrections during the class.

As she unrolled her mat, Hadley walked by and threw her a towel before heading over to greet more students who were now streaming in, mostly fake-tanned, fit twenty-somethings, some athletic-looking soccer moms, and a few men of varying ages. Neither Meara nor Jenny fit the status quo, but it didn't matter because Hadley liked everybody and everybody liked Hadley. That's why her studio slogan was: *A friend made on the mat is a friend for life.* The soft scent of lavender and the uplifting scent of ylang-ylang wafted through the air. Not only were they going to sweat out the toxins, but they were going to get some aromatherapy as well.

Meara sat cross-legged on her mat and Jenny sunk down to her knees. The question about Patrick and his possible incarnation as Greg was on the tip of her tongue, but as soon as she found the courage to ask—Hadley announced class was about to begin. There wouldn't be time to get all her answers during the class, so her growing list of questions would have to wait until afterward when they went to brunch.

Hadley took her place at the front of the room. Now she was wearing a headset and her voice was serene as she welcomed everyone to that morning's class, then gave some basic instructions before smiling.

"Let's begin with some standing pranayama."

∞

After contorting her sweaty body into twenty-six different poses, Jenny was happy when it was finally time to lay in corpse pose. That she could handle. She was also thankful for the towel because she had practically broken a wrist from all the sweat that had dripped onto her mat. How is it that people did this for *fun?* Finally, her breath became slow and even. Hadley brought them all back up to mountain pose and bowed to them in Namaste, thanking them for attending the class.

There was an ornate, shabby chic mirror near the bench and cubbies and Jenny got a glimpse of herself. Her entire face was flushed and pink, her hairline matted to her head in a disgusting, headband of hairy tendrils. She stole a glance at Meara, whose cheeks were rosy, but otherwise she had a healthy glow. If she admitted it though, she did feel like she released some baggage; she felt lighter if not spiritually, at least physically.

"Did you have a place in mind for brunch?" She shoved the towel into her bag to wash at home and tucked her mat under an arm. The hoodie was tied around her waist.

"Actually, there's a little vegan place that I love

not too far from here."

"Vegan?" That didn't sound too appealing. Jenny liked dairy. And meat. She definitely liked meat.

"Yeah, I'm a big believer in the energy my food absorbs. Don't worry, they have some vegetarian options too. If that's okay with you?" Food absorbing energy? And here she had thought Hadley was the *woo-woo* one. Apparently, Jenny was only beginning to dip her toe into the Ocean of Woo.

"Sure. Why not?"

They waved good-bye to Hadley and stepped out onto the sunny sidewalk. It wasn't as chilly as an hour ago and the warmth felt like an embrace across her bare shoulders. The two women took a minute to drop their yoga gear off into their cars, then walked along the sidewalk heading west. Meara explained that the restaurant was only a couple blocks away and that it wasn't exactly a restaurant, but a small five-table café style place attached to the owner's home. Cleveland wasn't necessarily hopping with trendy food options, but the owner was a friend of Meara's who had moved to Colorado for a time, and then came home with some new healthy habits.

The café was to the right of the house. Both were

painted a faded turquoise, and the café had a bright, coral colored door. It seemed cheerful enough. In pretty script the word *Faye* was hung above the door. Jenny assumed that was the name of both the friend and the café. The first thing Jenny noticed when they entered was how small it was. The second thing she noticed was how the sun filtered through the windows, making the small space seem like it was bathed in gold. It was quaint and felt warm and inviting.

"You choose a table. I'm going to find Faye and say hi. I'll be right back. Is coffee okay?"

"Yeah, coffee is great." Meara disappeared into a pair of swinging doors like in a saloon, except they were painted a cheerful yellow. There were two other patrons, an older man and woman sitting at a table on a small step up, just beneath a window. There were three tables beneath windows on the raised platform and two tables on the level Jenny was standing on. Every table had a small, white vase with what appeared to be fresh flowers. Near the door was what looked like an old dresser that had been refinished with coral-colored paint and then sanded to look old again. A very old looking cash register sat atop it, but then Jenny noticed the little white cube sitting beside it that was used to scan credit cards using a cell phone or tablet. Apparently, the cash register was just for show.

Jenny chose a table near a window, leaving an empty table in between herself and the older couple, who didn't seem to even notice her because they were so immersed in each other. Meara returned with two menus and two cups of black coffee. The menu was full of meat and dairy alternatives, as well as things with strange names like millet, amaranth, and quinoa. Luckily, Meara was good on her word and there were some vegetarian options, like eggs and baked items made with actual butter.

A short woman with  graying brown hair tossed over her shoulder in a thick braid came to the table. She was wearing an apron patterned with faded flowers. When she looked at Jenny her eyes were kind.

"Hi, I'm Faye, Meara's friend of way too many years!"

"If you keep serving food this good, Faye, you'll never get rid of me!"

Faye's smile widened. "Yeah, how many lifetimes now?" The two women laughed and Jenny didn't know if Faye was kidding or if she was serious. When the laughter ended, Meara ordered some kind of warm, grain cereal with fresh fruit. Jenny decided to stick with what she knew, and ordered two eggs, scrambled with a banana nut muffin. Faye assured them it wouldn't be long, before disappearing back behind the swinging doors.

Meara looked content as she took a sip of her coffee. Apparently, this was her element just as much as her office or the yoga studio. Jenny noticed the mugs were mismatched. Meara's was a giant, yellow smiley face, whereas hers was pale pink with a pale image of a butterfly.

"She collects mugs. Anywhere she goes or travels, Faye's always on the hunt for mugs to use in the café."

"You've known her a long time?" Jenny picked at the chipped nail polish on her thumb.

"More than one lifetime." Meara shrugged as if it were no big deal, and now, given what she knew, Jenny supposed it wasn't that big of a deal. It just *was.* As sure and real as the rise and set of the sun. "But enough about my lifetimes. Let's talk about yours."

# Chapter Thirty-Two

Meara was used to listening. It was 80% of her job description. Listen and then ask the questions that will help clients to find answers. She was also used to clients experiencing some residual memories, a flash of a smile here, or a feeling associated with a place that held a lot of emotion in a past life. Despite her twenty years working as a regression therapist, she had never had a client quite like Jenny McClain. Her past lives, and her present incarnation, were so tightly interwoven that it seemed as though a single frayed thread could somehow cause the whole thing to unravel.

Regressing to past lives was to help clients gain a better understanding of their present situations and to learn the ultimate lesson: having compassion for oneself.

Often it was easier to have compassion for other people—even complete strangers—than it was to have compassion for yourself. Meara sipped her second cup of coffee as Jenny explained the revelation about her mother and the connection to her behaviors in the present, how she suspected that Greg was possibly an incarnation of Evert and Patrick—even sharing the common name, but for some reason Erin's life seemed to still play softly in the background of Jenny's life.

"And you followed the directions I gave you?"

Jenny nodded vigorously, clearly frustrated. "I even painted."

Meara raised an eyebrow. "Painted?"

"After each regression I felt inspired to paint: Adala, Menodora, Erin…I've painted each of them. In my own way."

"That seems like a beautiful tribute. It sounds like you've done everything right." Meara took a sip of coffee. "It's very plausible about Greg, especially interesting that your mother introduced you, given her overwhelming drive to take care of you after experiencing several lives where she couldn't. Or felt that she couldn't. With Greg, there will come a time when you know—when you recognize his soul, and his soul recognizes yours—and when it happens, be sure to listen. It's not silly, and it's not foolish to believe in soulmates. It's your Higher Self acknowledging his Higher Self. Very few people are aware enough—open enough—to make the connection. So many people spend their lives with the wrong people because they didn't listen to their Higher Self and heed its direction."

Jenny nodded again. She felt drawn to Greg. He wasn't like the guys she usually dated. Instead, he was smart, funny, and kind. And if she were being honest with herself, that's all she truly wanted—all that she'd ever wanted, but for some reason—rebellion or denial—she would choose men who were the complete opposite of that. Maybe she wasn't the best version of herself in those moments; maybe Greg wouldn't have wanted to date her either. It was weird to think of it like that, as if the events of one's life were to some degree orchestrated beyond earthly control. Jenny thought of every person as concentric circles, moving in and out of each other's lives, learning a lesson, leaving an impression. All inter-connected. Life wasn't one, short linear existence. It was a series of existences—these short, fractured lives—that strung themselves together to form something even more meaningful than we could ever imagine in our own seemingly finite reality.

"I have a thought about why Erin's life has had such an impact on your current one."

Jenny was hopeful. As much as she enjoyed learning from Erin's existence—despite its tragic ending—the flashes of memory were at times overwhelming and even confusing. Despite being the same soul, Jenny still wanted to be living her life as herself, as Jennifer Eirene McClain. "Why?"

"The taxicab driver."

"But I already talked to my mother."

"Not Marvin. The other taxicab driver."

"The one who killed Erin?" Jenny felt her heartbeat quicken. She had asked about the impact of her life on others and she had been shown.

Meara looked sympathetic. "Maybe it's time to reach out, Jenny. Be the bigger person and even though it may not mean a damned thing to him, your forgiveness will mean something to his soul, even if he doesn't know it."

"Do you think that will help with the memories?"

"I can't say for sure, but it couldn't hurt. Sometimes the lessons we learn through regressions are as much for us as they are for someone else." Meara put a reassuring hand on top of Jenny's. "Your Higher Self said you knew him. What did you say his name was?"

"Kevin. Kevin Foley."

∞

Her MacBook sat on the kitchen counter. It was open to her e-mail inbox. Jenny paced the length of the small kitchen. Caddie laid on the floor beneath the window, her large brown eyes the only thing, besides the occasional ear prick, that moved as she watched Jenny.

She couldn't remember if she'd deleted the e-mail from Kevin. In a way it's what started all of this—the crazy journey of past life regressions. Sure, it was actually Hadley's idea, but Jenny's inability to move past their relationship as if she were somehow chained to it was the catalyst that drove her to find answers. And she had. Deep down she knew Kevin wasn't a bad person, at least she didn't think he was. She didn't even know him enough to know. Just as Adala hadn't really known Krischen before marrying him and similarly, Menodora didn't have her heart invested in a marriage to Nikomedes. Neither woman had really known either man. If Jenny thought about it she wasn't even sure she could name Kevin's favorite color or even his favorite food.

The last straw had been ditching her at her own art exhibition—her first real showcase—but, if she were being honest which now seemed to be her new standard operating procedure, she was as absent from Kevin's life as he had been from her own. Their paths had inextricably crossed for a short-time and Jenny was angry, more at herself than anyone, when it dead-ended. But there had to have been a reason. She knew now that those concentric circles were not randomized, that people entered one another's life with a purpose—either to help you or to provide a mirror for you to truly see yourself. The karmic connections were more than Jenny could understand, but clearly her soul needed to deliver a message to Kevin. And she knew just what that message was supposed to be, if not for his soul's evolution, but for her own.

She sighed and typed his name into the search bar in her inbox. It would pull up old messages still lingering in her inbox or messages she'd deleted since she hadn't cleaned out the trash folder. It only took a few seconds, but it felt like minutes as she watched the blue circle slowly rotate as it searched her folders. Finally, it pulled up a few messages. Two forwarded messages from Jenny to Kevin and one reply from Kevin, dated over a year ago. No one ever e-mailed anymore. Everything was done over text message or social media. The very top message was from Kevin. No subject line. A pet peeve, but it didn't surprise her. Kevin wasn't the follow-through type, his attention was forever moving on to the next best thing. He didn't have time for subject lines.

Taking in a deep breath, she clicked on it—the message she had been avoiding for months:

*Jenny, I know you probably aren't expecting an e-mail from me, but for some reason you've been on my mind. Not in the way that you're thinking. But...because I've been doing a lot of work on myself lately. You are probably thinking yeah, right, but it's true. I was mad at myself for the way that I treated you, and yet at the same time I felt like I couldn't help myself. I did love you, but felt a lot of anger toward you and didn't even know why. Even after you were no longer around, I still felt so angry, like the emotions could explode out of me at any second. Then a couple months ago, my car was in the shop and I had to take a taxi to run an errand. Another gentleman in my apartment complex also needed a taxi, so we decided to share it. Turns out he was on his way to church and long story short, his church sounded like nothing I'd ever heard of before: they read the Bible and other books about life and religion. They focused on humankind and the goodness in the world, and I thought 'Man, I could use some of that.' Only I'd said it out loud and before I knew it the old coot was inviting me to join him right then and there. The weirdest part is that I went. Somehow it changed me. I felt different, only I can't explain it. I know it sounds like something out of those lame Lifetime movies you would watch, but it was actually happening to me! Which leads me to the point of this e-mail. I'm heading to Central America with some other church members to spread word of the light of the Lord that resides in each one of us—not only when you are being 'good', but all of the time, especially when you're not. Basically, I wanted to say thank you. I see that my actions may have dulled your own light, and for that I apologize. I hope you are doing well. I understand if you don't reply. –Kevin*

It didn't sound like the Kevin she had known. He did indeed sound different. Just like Patrick and Erin, maybe Kevin was meant to share that taxicab that day, just as he had been destined to drive the one that killed Erin. And just as Jenny knew what she had to do in order to release the lingering memories of Erin's life—before it could start to overshadow her own. She hit the reply button.

*Kevin—It's amazing to hear that you are doing so well. Sorry it took me so long to reply, but I've been doing some work on myself as well. I think we were both angry that we didn't get what we wanted out of our relationship. But it just wasn't meant to work out in the way that we thought we wanted. I accept your apology and I forgive you. I hope you can do the same of me. Good luck in Central America. -Jenny*

She re-read it twice then took a deep breath before hitting the big, blue send button. For all she knew he could be in Central America already with no e-mail access, but that was okay, because it didn't really matter if he ever even saw her message. It was the intention of the message. Whether he realized it or not, Kevin seemed to be accepting his choices and their consequences on a deeper level, just as Jenny had realized that she needed to offer forgiveness to the one person she thought she could never give it to.

Again if she was being honest—which she was trying really hard to do more of—it felt good to e-mail Kevin. It offered closure and a sense of finality that hadn't been available to her for the past year. She closed the top of her MacBook and peered out the window. The weather wasn't quite as beautiful as it had been the other day. It was overcast and there was a slight dip in the temperature. Across the street, near the park, the wind rolled a pink, plastic shopping bag down the sidewalk. Typical Cleveland weather. Caddie would have no interest in going outside if it was cold or if it was raining. Jenny was pretty sure she had the most particular diva dog on the planet.

Not wanting to disturb the mutt's slumber, Jenny headed down the hallway to her art studio. Leaning against the window sill were the paintings—three different women looked back at her—they all had a similar slope to their jawline—but their eyes each told a different story. *What do my eyes tell?* Meara had asked her for permission to use parts of her sessions and her overall experience in the book she was working on, and Jenny had agreed to it. She felt changed by the experience—Jenny 2.0—and if it could help at least one other person, then she would consider it a victory.

The art studio had a tall bookcase, a piece too large to fit anywhere else. Jenny didn't read as much as she liked, so some of the shelves housed bottles of paints and cans of brushes. There was a framed picture here and there, but what caught her eye was the ornate, shabby chic mirror that was on the bottom shelf. Her mother had bought it for her on her last birthday. Ugh, that was another thing. Her birthday was only a week away. *Still broke, still single, and still stuck.* Well, maybe a little unstuck. And things with Greg seemed to be going well even though they hadn't scheduled a second date yet. She made a silent promise to herself to text him how much fun she'd had and see if he was interested in getting together again soon.

The mirror was heavy, but really cute. It just didn't fit into Jenny's earthy, world traveler décor. Not that she'd traveled the world, but a girl could dream. Then again, perhaps she had in her other lives. She smiled. At the time the gift had seemed a little bit like a slap in the face. Was her mother trying to tell her something about her appearance? But back then, she was constantly on the defensive. Now she was able to see the gift for what it was: her mother had seen it and liked it, thinking Jenny would like it too. That's it. Nothing more, nothing less.

She pulled it off the shelf and set it on the window sill, pulling up the stool she didn't usually sit on, but used to rest her paints. When was the last time she'd really seen herself? Like, truly looked—not just brushing her teeth or applying her make up. Her hair was wavy and brown, well-past her shoulders almost to her chest. She hadn't noticed because it was worn up almost all the time. Her face had thinned out a little and for the first time she noticed slight dimples near the corners of her mouth, the first indication of laugh lines. She had her father's nose, a little larger than she wanted to admit, and a bit pointy, but her eyes were all her mother's. The colors were almost identical—a deep, velvety brown—and the shape was somewhere between almond and round.

Maybe thirty wouldn't be so bad. She had learned a lot in her twenties, made a lot of mistakes, had some successes. But perhaps it was time to move on, time to embrace a new Jenny, one who wasn't caught up in petty things and one who was slower to react, and faster to love more deeply. There was a missing piece to her *Windows to the Soul* collection, as she'd come to think of it, and she knew what needed to be done.

She propped a fresh canvas up on her easel and gathered her paints and brushes. Outside, the clouds bellies' burst and the rain pounded on the roof of the apartment. Jenny listened contentedly, painting feverishly, struck with inspiration and periodically peering around the canvas to check her reflection in the mirror that was still propped beside the other paintings. So immersed in her work, she didn't even hear her phone ding with a voicemail from Greg asking if she was free that night and that he had a surprise for her. But that was okay because whenever she finished, the message would still be there and Greg would be anxiously awaiting her response on the other side of town, trying to distract himself with watching a basketball game or searching the internet for new ophthalmology periodicals.

When she finished painting, hours had passed, because she wanted to get it just right. She stepped back and looked at the face which was identical to her own. The eyes were soft with a hint of sparkle—she hadn't added it to be whimsical or cute; she felt that was truly what she had seen in her reflection in the mirror. The gaze that leveled with hers did not say broke, lonely, or stuck. The eyes staring back at her were just as strong, beautiful, and compassionate as the three other pairs that she'd already painted.  These eyes were different, they knew something that the others didn't. They said: *hope.* And hope could only come from acceptance, and acceptance could only come from forgiveness. All this time she'd been concerned about the so-called Butterfly Effect that her life had on everyone else's, not realizing that her own past lives had a similar—if not stronger—ripple effect on her own existence.

She carefully set the mirror back on the bottom bookshelf, reminding herself to hang it on the wall in the hallway later. Then she moved the still damp canvas to the end of the row on the window sill. Four women, one fractured life.

# Chapter Thirty-Three

Jenny wasn't a romantic type. Her ideal date would be hiking or staying in wearing pajamas and watching Netflix. But on occasion she could suck it up and do something that bordered on the couple-y side. Such as a double date at a winery with Greg, Hadley, and Jedd. It wasn't exactly her idea. She had been ecstatic to see Greg's number on her missed calls and then listened to his voicemail with bated breath. Then, after recovering from a burst of girlish, teenager giggles, she phoned him back. He'd mentioned he liked wine and it triggered something about Hadley mentioning a new winery in the vineyards forty-five minutes east of town. And before she knew it Greg was asking all about Hadley and suggesting that they all go on a double date to the winery. To her chagrin, Hadley had thought it was a fabulous idea. Even though it was only their third meeting (and second official date), Hadley was dying to meet the mysterious Greg who, according to Jenny, made frequent appearances in her other lives.

That's why on a Friday night, Jenny stood in front of her closet vexed as to what to wear. The weather was still cool, especially at night, and the vineyard was near the lake, so it would probably be even cooler. Hadley and Jedd would be there any minute, and then they would pick up Greg—who was still living with Edna about fifteen minutes east of Jenny's apartment, on the way to the winery.

Finally, she settled on a pair of skinny jeans, a dusty rose V-neck t-shirt, an olive-colored anorak jacket, and a pair of beige ballet flats. They weren't her Converse, but she figured she could dress it up a little more for a winery. She left her hair out of its regular bun, allowing it to tumble over her shoulders in loose waves. Hearing the text message ding from Hadley indicating they were waiting downstairs, she swiped on several coats of mascara before grabbing her leather cross-body bag, kissing Caddie on the head, and running down the stairs two at a time. When she reached the car she was slightly winded, and made a mental note to go for a run more often than her usual once a month.

"Hey, lady," Hadley greeted her from the passenger seat of Jedd's Volkswagon Jetta. Jedd nodded his greeting as Jenny scooted into the back seat, then she gave him the coordinates for Greg's house to plug into the GPS. Once they were on their way, Hadley turned toward the backseat and asked, "So, how have you been since your brunch with Meara?"

Jenny went with the honest answer, since she was trying to do that more anyways, who better than with her best friend? "Actually, really good. Ever since the regression sessions started, I've been painting a lot more. I think I might have a collection."

Jedd looked at her in the rear view mirror. "That's really awesome. I've seen a couple of the things you've painted for Hadley. You're really good. My favorite is the beach one Had has hanging in the living room."

Jenny felt her cheeks flush, it wasn't often these days that she heard a lot of praise for her work. "Thanks, Jedd."

"Anything else?" Hadley pressed as Jedd navigated down I-90, fighting off straggling commuters.

"She had some advice for me."

"Such as?"

"She said I should e-mail Kevin."

If Hadley was surprised, she hid it well. But for some reason Jenny didn't think many things about her surprised Hadley. Besides she'd had several lifetimes to figure out what made her tick. "Well, did you?"

"Who's Kevin?" Jedd asked.

"Jenny's ex. He was a jerk face. They dated for three years and then he stood her up at her own art exhibit opening. That was the beginning of the end, thank the Universe."

"Wow. That is shady," Jedd agreed. Normally, Jenny would jump to Kevin's defense. It wasn't his fault, it was her fault he wasn't interested in her art. Instead, she didn't say anything about it. She didn't feel the need to justify his actions, or her actions. For the first time in the last year, she felt nothing about it.

"Actually, he'd emailed me a couple months ago and I just never read it. But apparently, he's joined some kind of church and wanted to apologize for how he treated me and how our relationship ended, before he goes off on a mission to Central America."

"Huh. I suppose if someone tells me they see a pig fly by, I'd be less surprised. So, what did you say?"

"I basically just said good luck and that I forgive him." She didn't bother to add that she was forgiving him not just for his behavior in this life, but for the mistakes—and accidents—both of them made in their past existences.

"And?"

"What is this an Oprah interview?"

"How did you feel afterward?"

"I felt…peaceful. Happy. Excited." Jenny had to think about it. All these emotions had been percolating for several days. She hadn't had any glimpses of memories that weren't hers, but all bets could be off when Greg showed up. That seemed to be when they happened the most, when Greg was around. Jenny decided that was a good sign, maybe not a hundred percent confirmation Greg was the incarnation of Evert or Patrick, but she'd realized earlier that morning that it didn't really matter. Someday she would know if it was true, but if she believed he was her soulmate—could be her soulmate—then he would be, and really that was all that mattered. If she could be herself around him and he could love and accept her as she was—unlike any of the other guys she'd ever dated—then that was enough.

"Good. I told you, Meara's amazing. She knows what she's doing." Hadley grinned as Jedd got off the freeway and turned down a series of side streets. Jenny felt her heartbeat quicken and her palms grow sweaty as the GPS indicated that their destination was near. It was like being fifteen all over again and having her mom drop her and some lanky, pimple-faced boy off at the movies, except instead of her mom driving now it was her best friend's boyfriend. Luckily, Greg was waiting outside when Jedd pulled up. Unlike her own mother's antics, Edna apparently didn't feel the need to see her adult son off on his date.

Greg opened the car door and Jenny got a whiff of a fresh, clean smell mixed with just cut grass. It made her nerves dissipate just enough to give a proper greeting. He was wearing his glasses and had a five o'clock shadow, the sleeves of his blue-striped button down shirt were rolled to the elbows and he seemed at ease, which also made Jenny feel more comfortable. Introductions were made as Jedd navigated back to the freeway. The awkward first meeting and first date were behind them, and it felt natural to be sitting here, her knee pressed ever so slightly against his. Greg sunk back into the seat cushions, casually dropping an arm over Jenny's shoulders—he grinned. "New friends, new winery. It's going to be a good night."

∞

It turned out Greg was right. It was a good night. No, correction. It was a wonderful night. The best Jenny had had in a long time, almost longer than she was willing to admit even to herself. There was that honesty thing again. That night she laid in bed with Caddie curled up beside her, not even minding that Caddie had three-quarters of the bed and had pushed her almost to the edge. She replayed the night like a highlight reel in her head.

The winery had been beautiful. It was right on Lake Erie and the main building was a mix of log cabin and stone masonry. The outdoor patio spilled out onto a grassy knoll that at its bottom led to the lake. To the right were acres of grapes that provided the winery's signature beverage. They had taken the tour—which was interesting, but not really Jenny's thing. She didn't drink much these days and when she did, it was beer or bust. However, it was still cool to see how the wine was processed and barreled. The tour even had a corny name like *From Grape to Glass.* Afterward, they'd headed to the patio.

The spring sky was alit in shades of pink, purple, and indigo as the sun pulled a disappearing act over the lake, slipping below the horizon. The patio was ambient, decorated in little white, twinkling lights. There were potted plants everywhere, high-top wooden tables, outdoor sofas near a fireplace, and an acoustic band playing in the corner. They chose a table near the fireplace and ordered a bottle of wine and some appetizers for dinner.

Jenny felt warm, whether from the wine or something else, she wasn't totally sure. Hadley asked Greg probing questions that he fielded like a pro: What brought him back to the area? Was he happy with his work? Had he ever tried yoga before? Job transfer. Yes, he enjoyed helping people. And no, he hadn't, but if Hadley was offering he was willing to try a class. Greg had remained unruffled, and Hadley had raised an appreciative eyebrow at Jenny over her wine glass.

Then the conversation turned to Hadley and Jedd. They told Greg the story of how they had met, and Jedd let on that they were talking engagement soon—a short one and possibly a fall wedding. This didn't surprise Jenny in the least. She was happy that her best friend had found her soulmate. Hadley wasn't a huge fan of surprises, a lavish engagement scheme would not be something she'd like or want. The quickness of it—six months or so—also didn't surprise Jenny. As Hadley had put it: "When you meet the one you want to spend the rest of your life with, you want the rest of your life to start as soon as possible." And, yes, of course she would be Hadley's maid of honor. She made Hadley pinky swear she would not choose any unflattering colors or fabrics for her bridesmaid dresses.

Inevitably though the conversation turned to Jenny and her life. Jedd was the one who had brought it up. "Jenny, didn't you say that you just finished a new collection?"

Jenny had almost choked on her wine, but she managed to quickly recover. "Yeah. Not my usual though."

"What's your usual?" Greg had asked. The fire reflected in his glasses, but Jenny could still see that his eyes were curious, not judgmental.

"Her usual are these really, beautiful, realistic landscapes," Hadley answered for her.

"Sometimes they're things I've really seen, but other times it's a combination of my experience and my imagination. But this time...this time I felt drawn to something different."

Greg had smiled, genuinely interested. "Tell me more."

"Well, I, uh...had some experiences recently that were...life altering. In a really, really good way. And I painted the faces of these women who influenced me...during this experience." Jenny knew it wasn't the whole truth, but she wasn't totally comfortable yet telling Greg she'd seen a Regression Therapist.

"Do you have any pictures of these paintings?" he'd asked. And actually, she did. After she had added herself to the quartet of paintings, she'd carefully used her iPhone to take photos of each individual painting. It didn't do them justice really, but she had wanted to show Hadley. She leaned in, her shoulder pressed against Greg's, and swiped her finger through the photo gallery of the paintings on her phone.

"The eyes..." he mumbled.

"...are the windows to the soul," Jenny finished. Then she had a brief recollection of a conversation they'd had the day they met. "I mean, the window to the universe."

Greg smiled. "That's right. As unique as fingerprints. No pair like any other. Each pair is unique. Just like the individual."

"Just like the soul," Hadley had added.

"A physical manifestation of our physical, spiritual, and emotional self." Greg had turned then to her, his gray eyes intense and Jenny could see so much inside them. She saw confidence and trust, hope and love, old wounds and second chances. They were both familiar and unknown to her at the same time. There was a flash of recognition—she saw it—just the minutest of sparkle in his eyes—but he shook his head and they were gone. Later, much later, she would ask him about that moment, and what he had seen in her gaze. And his answer would be simple. *Home*. He continued, "You know, I have a friend. He owns a gallery in one of the up-and-coming areas of town. His place is part art gallery, part art studio. I think he would love these. In fact, I am sure he would love these. Would you be willing to showcase them?"

Jenny was shocked. "Yes. Yes, of course! I would love to showcase them!"

"I'm actually going to be seeing him this weekend for the Tribe game. I'll run it by him and see what he says. He's been trying to draw in more patrons to the art gallery side—that's his true passion, he even has some of his own art displayed, but he loves to showcase local artists. Would you be willing to take part in a meet-the-artist type of event?"

Actually, Jenny hated social situations and being the center of attention, but despite her reservations the words tumbled out of her mouth before she could stop them. "That would be amazing!"

"Great!" Greg had said, placing a hand gently on her thigh, a jolt of warmth shooting through her. "I think he'll find them magnificent." And even though she knew he was talking about her paintings, the way he looked at her right then, with the moonlight shining down on his dark hair, his face aglow in amber, it felt like he was saying that *she* was magnificent. Maybe she was. It had just taken several lifetimes to see.

## Chapter Thirty-Four

*Butterflies are normal,* Jenny tried to tell herself. Caddie watched from atop the queen-sized bed's pillows. Jenny was pretty sure the dog found her struggles amusing. At the foot of the bed, several dresses were strewn about. There was the plum-colored one she'd worn to a friend's wedding a year ago, but when she put it on she had discovered a hole in a seam. *No time to fix it.* Then there was her LBD—little black dress—that hugged her in all the right places. Well, at least it used to. Now it seemed to have shrunk. Or Jenny seemed to have grown. *Let's not talk about that.* The last dress laying on the bed in a heap was a sundress, but it was denim. And a sundress. Not an art exhibit-opening-dress. Jenny flopped onto the bed feeling her eyes beginning to well up with tears. *It was her birthday damn it and she would cry if she wanted to.* Caddie licked the palm of her hand, which had landed near the dog's face. At least Caddie didn't care about her dress dilemma.

Her phone buzzed in her jeans pocket, she pulled it out and put it to her ear. "Happy birthday, Bestie." Hadley's voice sang in her ear.

"That's like the fifth time you've wished me a happy birthday. I already got your card yesterday, your e-mail this morning, and your text message this afternoon."

"That's only four."

"Oh, and the airplane with the banner that flew over my apartment just a little bit ago."

"You made that up. But it's a good idea. I'll take note for future birthdays."

"Funny."

"I'm just happy you're happy and that this is the day your parents did the wild monkey dance that brought you—uniquely you—into this world."

"Hadley, that's disgusting."

"It's the truth. So are you ready for tonight? Art exhibit in T minus three hours." And she had to be there an hour before the show started, to meet Greg's friend—the gallery owner—and to set up her paintings. Luckily,

Greg had offered to pick her up in his Jeep and help transport the paintings. So, she had two hours to eat some dinner (these types of events always made her ravenous), shower, and get dressed. Only, that was the problem. There was no dress.

"I have nothing to wear. I'm having a dress emergency. It's either too small, too casual, or has a big hole in it." She didn't mean for her voice to inflect with panic, but it was hard to disguise.

"I'll be there in thirty minutes."

∞

The hot shower somewhat calmed her nerves, but not completely. She and Hadley were almost the same size and she only hoped that she'd have a dress that could work. The door was unlocked and she didn't hear Hadley come in because of the blow dryer, so she nearly jumped out of her skin when Hadley appeared in the bathroom doorway. Hadley was wearing a long-sleeved maxi dress in a chocolate brown, her blonde waves were piled on her head and large gold, filigreed earrings dangled from her earlobes. She looked the epitome of *boho*-chic. In one hand she held two hangers with dresses and in the other she held a pizza from their favorite local place.

"I figured you'd be hungry. You always get

nervous before these things and there's always little to no food at them. I thought I'd save you the trouble."

"You're the best." Jenny replied as she went into the kitchen to grab paper plates and napkins before following Hadley back into the bedroom. Caddie lifted her head and sniffed the air as Hadley set the pizza box on the dresser. Double cheese and mushroom—both their favorite. If the shower didn't completely calm her nerves, the pizza definitely would.

Before Hadley took a slice of pizza she held up the two dresses, while Jenny ate. "I think these two should fit you. You're a little bigger on top than me, but we're about the same waist size." The dress on the hanger in her right hand was simple, red, and knee length. The other dress was a bit of a peasant style, with longer sleeves and looked slightly shorter than the other one. It had a blue background and a tiny, white floral print. Neither was really her style, but either was better than going naked at this point.

Jenny finished off her second slice of pizza then scooped up the dresses. She tried the red one on first and put an obi belt around the waist. Hadley examined her, frowning. "It's okay, but it's a little…plain. Try the second one." Obeying, Jenny undid the obi belt then slipped the red dress back over her head, exchanging it for the blue one. "Maybe, but it's missing something." The dress fit her well and when she looked in the mirror she thought it flattered her hair and skin tone, which was on the pale side since it wasn't quite summer yet. Hadley disappeared into the closet then came out with a handful of things. First she handed Jenny a cardigan, but then immediately made her take it off. Then she had her put on a brown leather jacket that hit just above the hips. She nodded. "Here, try these." Jenny slipped into a pair of nude-colored pumps, but Hadley shook her head. "Try the boots."

Hadley had an eye for fashion, unlike Jenny who often felt like a kid playing dress up. It was one part lack of knowledge and two parts lack of effort. That's why she would never think to pair the dress with a leather jacket and knee high brown boots. But it was perfect. It wasn't too casual and not too dressy. It was trendy and yet comfortable at the same time. And she felt like herself. Except better. Hadley nodded approvingly.

"Bam! That's what I'm talking about, Jenny 2.0." She grabbed a slice of pizza and took a big, cheesy bite. "Now, what are we going to do with that hair?"

∞

The gallery owner was in his mid-twenties, with slicked back hair and a handlebar mustache. He had on black, geek-chic eyeglasses and a fitted t-shirt that spelled out Love, but where the "O" should be, was the outline of the state of Ohio. Over his home-pride t-shirt, he had on a fitted blazer. His name was Abraham, but he said, "Call me Abe."

Abe, Greg, and Jenny arranged her quartet of paintings on the main gallery wall, starting with Adala then placing Menodora, Erin, and the self-portrait to the right. Jenny felt it was important that the paintings progress from what she knew was lifetime to lifetime, ending with herself. At least for now. The gallery was small, which gave the paintings the advantage of filling the single wall they were displayed on. Little lights hung above each painting.

"You know," Greg said standing back and studying the paintings as Abe went to greet the caterer for the evening's exhibit. "These women look familiar."

Jenny felt her blood freeze. Was it possible that Greg had figured out who she truly was? Figured out who he was to her? "They do?"

"Yes. If I didn't know better, I'd say they're all the same woman."

"That's impossible. They're clearly different women. Their facial features are different and their hair color. That one over there, she has a strong German jawline, and the one over there, she has a lot more freckles than any of the others."

"But the eyes." He turned and looked down at her, placing a hand affectionately around her waist. "The eyes on the left, they're strong and maybe a bit foolish," he squinted to view the tiny plaque that Jenny had provided which read *Adala by Jennifer McClain* beneath it. "Perhaps Adala was known to act before thinking. And then Menodora, she looks younger than Adala, but her eyes, tell a different story. There is the same naivety, and yet she seems almost regal. Her eyes say that she has seen horrible things, but beautiful things too." He squinted looking at the third painting. "And then Erin, her eyes tell of worldly travels and have the sparkle of unconditional love."

"You got all that from my paintings?" Jenny whispered.

"Of course. I wasn't lying when I said you're very good."

"What about the last painting?" Jenny had named this one differently. She had used her middle name,

Eirene, because it meant *peace*. And that's how she felt now. At peace with herself, with where she had been, where she was, and where she was going. The feeling had been unfamiliar, but now it was comforting like her favorite blanket that smelled just like Caddie.

"Ah, that one's my favorite," he leaned into her with a chuckle. "But if I'm being honest this woman is much wiser than the other three. Not only is there still a hint of innocence, but she has clearly seen things both good and bad. Maybe she has experienced great love, but also experienced great hurt. And yet, there's a knowing sparkle to her eye that she realizes everything is going to work out just fine because it always does. She looks at the viewer of the painting head on, almost boldly, as if she is ready for anything, but at the same time there's a quiet serenity about her." While he was talking Greg had turned, and instead of staring at the painting, he had both hands on Jenny's waist and was staring down at her.

Jenny realized then, he didn't know who she was. And it still didn't matter. What mattered is that he knew who she was in this moment, in this lifetime. Her voice was barely above a whisper. "That's what Eirene means, peace."

"It's a fitting title," he mumbled and for the first

time he leaned down and placed his mouth on hers. It wasn't a sloppy, lusty kiss like the ones she was used to from ex-boyfriends, this time it was the cliché. *It was different.* She felt the warm bubbles of excitement float through her body. Maybe it wasn't that the kiss was different, maybe it was that *she* was different. It ended too quickly, but Jenny knew there was time for more of that later—a lifetime for it. "I have something for you."

Greg disappeared inside a small room which served as Abe's office and returned with a package. It was wrapped in brown paper. "I know it's not wrapped all pretty and stuff, but happy birthday."

"How'd you know?"

He gave her an impish grin. "Hadley."

Jenny laughed as she began to carefully remove the package's tape. "Of course." She unfurled the brown paper and inside was a loosely folded piece of canvas. Greg helped her unfold it and then took it from her holding it up, so that she could read the sign he'd had designed for her, just for this art exhibit. In beautiful script it read: *Windows to the Soul: An Artistic Meditation of the Universe by Jennifer McClain.*

"It's lovely!" Jenny breathed. "How did you decide what to name it?" After all, he'd only originally seen the paintings on her cell phone, not in person.

"I had a feeling, based on what you showed me and our conversations."

"I think it's perfect."

Because Jenny now knew the deeper truth behind such a seemingly innocuous statement. Each of these past lives, these glimpses she had been fortunate enough to experience, gave the world a unique perspective. One that only each woman—and no one else—could provide. Just as Greg had observed. Each woman gained life lessons that contributed to the development of the same soul. It could be tragic at times, but now Jenny saw that there could be hope born from those same tragedies. Being broke or single wasn't the end of the world. In fact, nothing was, because she knew her soul would go on forever, continuing to learn its lessons and share its wisdom about accepting, forgiving, experiencing unconditional love, and finding the silver lining in what seemed like otherwise impossible circumstances. She found unexpected comfort in the fact that life wasn't short and finite as she'd previously believed, but instead it was long and infinite, filled with tiny fractures that shape the identity of each soul. It didn't matter who she was or who she had been, all that mattered was who she was now in this moment. Because it was always changing. And it would continue to do so for all of time. Because time was all that any of us truly had.

And that was the beauty of it.

## ACKNOWLEDGEMENTS

I was inspired by two books before and during the writing of *The Fractured Life of Jenny McClain*. Mira Kelley's *Beyond Past Lives* is what really got my wheels turning about regression therapy and what it means about our existence. I then read *Miracles Happen: The Transformational Healing Power of Past-Life Memories* by Kelley's mentor Dr. Brian L. Weiss and his daughter, Amy Weiss. I've always believed that there is something more to this world and these books provide me with both reassurance and curiosity. I highly recommend reading them if you'd like to explore the topic further. I'd also like to thank my dad for editing and Shannon for reading. I'm pretty sure this isn't the first life we've crossed paths!

## ABOUT THE AUTHOR

Jennifer L. Kelly is a middle childhood educator. She resides in Cleveland, Ohio. When she isn't writing, she can be found fangirling over *Doctor Who,* doing yoga, spending time with her dog, or reading. She is the author of the YA series *The Lucia Chronicles* and the upcoming *The Elementals series*. Visit her website ***Skim.Scheme.Scribble:*** ***www.jenniferlkelly.com*** Or say *HI!* :

***info@jenniferlkelly.com***

***JenniferLKelly3***

***AuthorJenniferLKelly***

***AuthorJenniferLKelly***

www.ingramcontent.com/pod-product-compliance
Lightning Source LLC
Chambersburg PA
CBHW030525310726
48979CB00010B/1808/J

*9780997776409*